Ouroboros

Nicholas Unger

BeachhouseBooks

Saint Charles Missouri USA

Cover design by Robert J. Banis, PhD, fderived from
graphics designated as Public domain gathered from the
site Wikipedia.org. the cover image was derived from a
Drawing by Theodoros Pelecanos, in a 1478 copy of a lost
alchemical tract by Synesius, reproduced at Wikipedia.org

ISBN 9781596301016
Library of Congress Control Number: 2016900846

BeachHouse
Books

www.beachhousebooks.com

an Imprint of
Science & Humanities Press
Saint Charles MO 63301
(636) 394-4950

Monday, January 15ᵗʰ, 60 days left

Aiden had a knife in his pocket. His fingers were lightly curled around the blade. He waited for his target on a park bench. A flowing river ran before him. Blocks of ice bobbed in and out of the surface like ice cubes in a glass. He looked at his reflection in the stream. Aiden was a skinny, gangly figure with a mangled mug and a twisted nose that had been broken years ago in a bar fight. His thick black hair grew around his face like moss on a stone and several teeth were missing in his smile. *You do what you do because you look like this.* Aiden shook his head like a dog climbing out of a pool. A woman walked by with a poodle, and then silence. It was cold out, but the cool air must have felt good when you were exercising. It was a good day for a run. It was peaceful and there weren't too many people around. It was a nice place for a kill.

Aiden's target was a prosecutor. Aiden had acquired many skills over his career. He could snipe the man from afar. He could cut the breaks on his vehicle, but every person was different, and it all depended on when they were most vulnerable. Everybody was vulnerable at some point. Presidents have been killed by regular citizens. All you need is the right opportunity. Aiden had studied his target well. He knew where the man lived; he knew where the man worked. He knew his daily habits. The man's name was Kevin, and he liked to jog late in the evening.

The sun was hovering above the horizon, its gaze breaking through the trees. The yellow glow was dim. The world was washed in a blue hue. Kevin was a large man. He carried a gun. He was a man whose chin always pointed up. The man grew up in the north, the nicest section of the city, dozens of gated communities and quiet suburbs. Anybody living in the north could be forgiven for being ignorant of the violence in the south despite being residents of the same city. When Aiden was growing up he had a deep resentment for the richer kids. He hated the fact that their lives were so much easier than his. His relationship with his employer Bartley didn't remedy his resentment. You belong here with us. You have a family here Aiden remembered Bartley telling him. Bartley owned a bar close to where Aiden grew up. Aiden would visit the place every day after school. It was better than going home and seeing his father drown himself in alcohol.

Aiden checked the time on his flip phone. The prosecutor would be here soon. Aiden stretched back on the bench. He heard a couple bones crack. His back was always sore. Aiden took out a bottle of pills. He swallowed two painkillers. It was the middle of January and there was still a thin layer of snow on the ground. On the other side of the river were more woods. Aiden knew there was a bridge that crossed the river further down the trail, but he had never been to the other side.

Aiden waited patiently. He was good at waiting. He heard footsteps behind him and he turned his head. He saw a man, but it wasn't his target. The man Aiden saw was young, thin, and had a long face. The young man walked over, and Aiden's fingers tightened around his blade. The young man sat down after brushing off snow from his seat. He took out a cigarette from the pack in his coat pocket. He offered Aiden a smoke, but Aiden refused.

"Don't smoke?"

"No."

The young man shrugged and put the cigarette in his own mouth. He shivered and rubbed his arms.

"God damn is it cold... You know, I never really liked hiking."

"That so?"

"Wife made me go. Says it's better for my health. I've been going to the gym, been eating salads. It's not really the reason I have no endurance."

The young man took the cigarette out of his mouth. He examined it. The burning ember on the end was slowly fading. He flicked it into the river.

"She doesn't know. Knows there's something wrong, but nothing specific. You know how to keep a secret?"

"No."

The young man shrugged. He seemed to be talking more to himself. Aiden sighed and rubbed his forehead. He had a migraine so he took a painkiller.

"What's that?"

"Medication… sore back."

"I got, um…what'd they say… Hyperactivity! I just think I'm an extrovert. You think I talk too much?"

"Yes."

"I take pills for it. Don't want to. I'd like to deal with this on my own. You think I'm being sensitive?"

"I don't know."

Why can't he take the hint? Aiden looked around. When would the prosecutor be here? Aiden looked at the time on his phone. Only a couple of minutes had passed. It felt like it had been a half hour. Aiden groaned. The young man didn't stop babbling.

"Work at a retail store. Stand for hours at a time, but maybe the reason I'm so worked up is because I'm so overworked. I don't need medication. Whose making you take your pills?"

"Me."

"Oh, well... you're lucky. You just got to worry about yourself. I wish I were you."

Aiden listened to the rushing water. He focused on the sound and he hoped perhaps it would drown out the sound of the young man's voice.

"... Do you have a dog? They're great animals. I have a bulldog. I love the face of those animals. They have a lot of health problems but..."

Aiden looked behind himself; still no prosecutor? Aiden thought of ways to get rid of the young man. The most obvious solution was to kill him, but he didn't want to deal with two bodies. Disposing of one was hard enough. Nobody else had walked on the trail since the young man had come. Aiden sighed. He decided he might as well become invested in the conversation. Maybe if he talked a little the young man would be satisfied and leave.

"Do you have kids?"

The young man stopped talking. Aiden had interrupted him, but that wasn't why he was suddenly quiet. He looked down at his feet.

"My girl wants to start a family. I'm not so sure. I love kids, but I'm worried how good a father I would be. Do you have kids?"

Aiden shook his head.

"What was your father like?"

"... I never knew my father."

"My father ran from us when I was young. I don't want to suggest that's where my fear is coming from. I'm seeing a psychologist and that's what he keeps telling me."

The young man stood up. He took out his empty pack of cigarettes and threw the carton into the river. He took out his lighter and looked like he was going to chuck that away too. He stopped and looked at it. It was a cheap blue dollar store lighter. He had endearment in his stare. He looked at the river.

"I shouldn't pollute the water like that."

"I think it's polluted already."

"Nevertheless..."

The young man tossed the lighter into Aiden's lap.

"You can keep it, but I'm not going to need it."

"Can't you throw it out before you leave the park?"

"Yeah, but... consider it a token. I hope to see you again."

The young man stuck out his hand. Aiden was hesitant, but he shook it.

"I'm James."

"John."

"I hope to see you again."

"That would be nice."

Aiden gave a closed smile. The young man started to walk away. Aiden knew he would never see the young man again. He looked at the lighter. He could throw it into the river, but he put into his pocket. He thought he would get rid of it later. He heard footsteps. Had the young man forgotten something? Was he coming back? Aiden turned around and he could see a large man running. He was tall, at least six feet. Aiden was five nine. The man was in sweat pants and a hooded sweat shirt. He had massive arms. He had a handgun stuffed in the back of his pants. Aiden stood. He started running behind the man. The prosecutor turned around. His eyes grew wide. He could tell there was something wrong with Aiden. He reached for his gun, but Aiden was already close.

He took out his knife. He pushed it underneath Kevin's chin. He pushed the blade deeper. Kevin's body was still for a moment before slumping sideways and falling to the ground. Aiden remained calm. His heartbeat was steady. Aiden kneeled down next to Kevin. The eyes were wide open, staring back. He grabbed the man's two large hands and began to drag him to the water's edge. Aiden's back burned. He grunted and continued to pull Kevin's heavy bulk. He kicked the body into the river.

Aiden watched the body float a few feet away before finally sinking. Aiden wondered for a moment how long the prosecutor's body would remain undiscovered. He looked behind him at the cement path that wormed its way through the park. He guessed it was close to eight. More people would be coming. Aiden kneeled down, cupped his hands together and splashed some of the frigid water on his hands and face. Aiden washed the blood off the blade.

He turned around and saw the prosecutor's wallet hidden among the dead leaves. He picked it up. There was a picture inside. Aiden looked at two girls. The nine year old was chubby, and the fifteen year old had braces. They certainly looked very happy in the photograph with bright enthusiastic smiles. They were both brunettes. Their long hair braided into pony tails. The younger one had two pony tails while the older girl had a single long strand running down the back of her neck. He threw the wallet in the river. He put the photograph in his pocket. *You know you're going to hell.* I know. It was still snowing.

Aiden lived in a motel in a rundown part of town. Young half naked girls walked the streets and druggies walked around muttering to themselves. Aiden knew a few of the girls, and they knew he never wanted their services. Aiden just wanted to get to bed as quickly as possible. His room was a cramped messy fit in the left wing of the complex. Everything seemed lumped together; the television, the bed, and the dresser where he kept his clothes. They all consumed what little space was available. The maid service was horrendous. They rarely changed the bed and never vacuumed. These chores were all left up to Aiden to complete.

The price to live at the motel was low, and Aiden loved the fact that he could get up and go anytime he wanted. Aiden crawled into his bed which was cleaner than it was most nights although he knew he would have to wash the sheets sometime soon. He turned on the massive television set in front of him. It was an old boxy TV that looked like it weighed about three hundred pounds, but Aiden received only three channels. The only channel that really interested him was the local news.

The top story was on the rising crime rates. Several different atrocities had been committed over the week. A man was murdered on the Southside near Aiden's motel. The police claimed the perpetrator was a Black. Aiden acted as a representative once for Bartley Collins when he initiated a pact between the Blacks and Bartley's gang when Bartley went to war with the Russians. Aiden remembered that war. He nearly got torn in half in a drive-by while walking down the street. He still got the jitters sometimes when he heard a car pull up behind him.

Aiden stopped reminiscing and went to the bathroom, but he shivered when he entered. The room was freezing. Aiden watched a slender insect with wispy legs float over the greasy tiles. Aiden thought about killing the creature, but it found a crack in the wall to hide in. Aiden looked at himself in the mirror. He always seemed to be looking at himself, and it wasn't from vanity although he was intrigued by his own appearance. He had an interesting face that he couldn't believe was his own. He looked like a mangy stray dog. His hair was a thick matted mop that nearly covered his eyes. Aiden was in his late forties, and his hair was starting to grey.

Aiden brushed his teeth. The few left were hanging on for dear life. Aiden recounted how he had lost them. Many went missing after the fights he had and a couple he lost when he was an adolescent because they became infected. Aiden spit out the toothpaste that was in his mouth. He figured flossing at this point was useless. Aiden took some painkillers. He took the painkillers to relieve himself, and when he discovered they were useful in relieving other ailments he began taking painkillers whether his back was sore or not although he had been warned not to take too many.

Aiden ran the bathwater. He checked the temperature, but it was warm enough and the room soon began to steam like a sauna. He undressed. His body was skeletal and he had knobby joints. He smiled when he thought about how terrifying his silhouette was. He must have looked like the boogeyman. He had one tattoo. Ouroboros was drawn over his left breast. It was an ancient symbol. Most of the boys when Aiden was young adopted it because it looked cool: a snake that ate itself, forming a circle. They insisted he get it too, but he didn't figure he needed to decorate his skin since his back looked like a checker board. Bruises and scars covered his body. Aiden slowly descended into the warm water. He felt so tired. He felt like he was already in bed beneath his covers.

Things would get better. They would have to, right? All this pain and suffering he felt all the time couldn't have been for nothing. Aiden shook his head again. He drained the tub and put on a pair of clothes; he got into bed and shut his eyes, and thought about his mother. She died when he was young. He couldn't remember her well. He could still see her face. He could still see her smile in his head, but he couldn't remember much else about her. He couldn't rely on his father to tell him what she was like, but perhaps that was for the best. He didn't want to break his fantasy, his conception of a perfect parent. He didn't want that to be shattered. It always took him a while before he started to doze. Aiden stared at the ceiling. His thoughts were relentless. A spring pierced through the mattress and jabbed him in the side. He threw off his covers.

Aiden went back to the bathroom. He grabbed his bottle of painkillers. He sat next to the toilet. Aiden waited with the bottle open. There was water on the floor from the bath. He stared at his reflection in the pool. Would this be how he went? He kept waiting not sure how long it was possible to just sit there. Aiden thought about the first man he ever killed. It was such a strange, cold feeling like being splashed with ice water. Aiden heard a buzzing in his ear. He looked around him, but saw nothing. The man had had a daughter Aiden later discovered. The first man he killed. It was always a struggle with him. He didn't know how much he wanted to know about those he hurt or who their loved ones were. Aiden kept thinking of the prosecutor's daughters. He shook his head. He took out the picture. He took out the lighter. He had forgotten he had it. He burned the two girls.

Tuesday, January 16th, 59 days left

Aiden had fallen asleep. His head was resting on the toilet lid. It was almost lunchtime when he opened his eyes. He put the blue lighter on the rim of the sink. He got up and got dressed. He needed to collect his payment from Bartley. He walked outside. The girls on the sidewalk had all disappeared. You still heard the occasional gunshot and police sirens in the distance, but it didn't appear too dystopian. Aiden felt good or as good as he ever felt. The sun was shining, and it was a particularly warm day for the month of January.

Bartley's Bar wasn't far away. Aiden decided to walk. He was embarrassed to drive his car, a beat-up station wagon held together by duct tape. The windshield on Aiden's vehicle was smashed, and the inside smelled like gas. Aiden used to live in a house before the motel that was heated by oil, but one night when Aiden had run out he picked up some kerosene that spilled all over his backseat. The walk didn't take too long. The bar was inconspicuously located between two much larger buildings and the entrance was around back guarded by an intimidating looking bouncer who let him through without even glancing down at the clipboard he was holding.

"Thanks Mike."

The bouncer nodded back.

The bar was dimly lit inside. There was a small band playing quiet jazz in the corner and near the band were several tables one of which seated Bartley. He was sitting with several other men Aiden didn't know. A couple of those men were uniformed police officers. Bartley didn't even acknowledge Aiden when he sat down. He was too focused on the trumpet player. Bartley pointed at the man as he started to go into an in-depth solo piece.

"He's good."

Bartley had a matter of fact way of speaking, even about things he enjoyed. Aiden didn't know. He never listened to Jazz. There weren't many people in the bar; fifteen, including the people who served, listened to the music.

"Why don't you play Irish music?"

"Everybody listens to Irish music in this city; I need to stand out somehow."

"I thought you did everything in your power not to stand out."

"Caution is always advisable, but in this city it doesn't really matter."

Aiden shrugged. Bartley was a fat balding imp with a pug nose and round spectacles that made his eyes look like huge saucers. His huge gut hung over his belt like a fleshy avalanche. How a man like him had acquired so much power was a mystery to most, but Aiden knew Bartley was ruthless, calculating, and intelligent. He schemed constantly, and Aiden knew better than to get on his bad side. Bartley turned around to give Aiden his attention. He smiled.

"Have you heard about that prosecutor? How awful. It was all over the news this morning. Apparently he was mugged walking home from work. The poor man was shot and dumped in the river."

Several men, including the police, snickered. Aiden's face was placid.

"Still no sense of humor?"

"Do you have my money?"

Bartley tossed over a white envelope. Aiden lifted up the flap and peaked. There were several dozen hundred dollar bills.

"I have to go."

"Where do you have to go exactly?"

"I would like to leave unless you have any more work."

"I do have something for you…"

Aiden waited, but before Bartley could finish a waitress came over and put drinks down on the table.

"Thank you, dear… There's this reporter working for a local newspaper. He's been a real thorn in my side. If you could deal with this problem I would be exceptionally grateful."

"How grateful?"

"I haven't checked my balance recently, but I might be able to part with ten thousand."

Aiden thought for a moment. There was something he didn't like about attacking a reporter. He didn't even like killing the prosecutor. Yet he could see the prosecutor as his enemy. Aiden was a criminal and he separated himself from the police. The prosecutor might not have worn a blue uniform, but nonetheless he was in the same ballpark, but a reporter was too close to being a civilian. Then again, money was money. Bartley tossed over a photograph. Aiden picked it up and put it in his pocket without looking at it. Bartley's smile grew.

"I'll call you."

"One more thing: I got a kid I'd like you to meet. He's a good kid. It won't cause you too much trouble. I'll throw in an extra bonus."

Aiden continued walking, but Bartley knew Aiden would accept. He had nothing else to do. Every day was the same routine. He woke up; he went to Bartley's bar to see if there were any jobs available. If there were, like today, then he would go home and sleep. Getting as much rest as he could before he had to go out and kill or maim somebody's father or brother or son. If there wasn't a job available... Aiden would go home and sleep. He had no idea what else to do or where to go, so off he went back to the motel.

It was mid-afternoon and he hated the fact that he already wanted to take a nap. He put his envelope of money under his mattress. There he kept weapons and a contact list. There were several envelopes near the one Bartley had recently given him. He earned enough money to move out of the Southside, but he didn't know how well he would live in the North or even among the working class. He could buy himself a new car. He might even be able to quit. There were a lot of things he could do.

He sat down on the bed and watched the news. There was a story on about the prosecutor who was shot in the park, but not much information was given other than the fact that it was some black who robbed him late at night. The news lady had used the term... of African-American descent. Aiden turned off the television. He got off his bed and went to the bathroom. He grabbed the bottle of painkillers and he sat next to the toilet. He wondered if today would be the day. He waited. The silence was frightening. The water that had been on the floor last night dried up. Aiden watched an insect with wispy legs float across the floor. Was it the same one he had seen before? Aiden closed the pill bottle. He didn't know what had come over him. He had a burst of energy similar to anger. He grabbed a paper towel. He picked up the insect and rushed it outside. He went back into his room and started to get dressed.

Before, Aiden had resisted the pills out of laziness, and it had to be one of the poorest excuses not to commit suicide. He just figured he would put it off another day and see if things got better, but they never did. He was tired of waiting. *I'm going out. I'm going to try. If anything bad happens then I'll quit, but I have to try.* There was a separate thought: *when was the last time you have been out? Actually went out and had fun; A decade, Two decades, Twenty years?* Jesus. Had it been so long? Aiden shook his head. He put on a red shirt and jeans. He went quickly to the bathroom to check himself. He smiled. He looked like a caveman that somebody had brought to the future.

It was early so Aiden decided to walk to the North side. He needed the exercise anyhow. He went through the park. Not many people were there, probably because they had heard about the mugging of the prosecutor on the news. Aiden thought it was hilarious that the public had no idea who they should be truly afraid of. Aiden never even carried a gun except when he was on a job. He kept walking. He tried searching for a bar he had never been to. The sky was graying by the time he reached the North side. He knew he would have to make a decision soon. He eventually ended up at a familiar place called the Northeastern Tavern. Its wooden exterior was severely aged. Aiden saw the date of construction was in the eighteenth century.

It was a small but quaint looking place. It was built at a time when there were more woods. The former industrial section on the Westside replaced the forest. Not every part of the north was a nice place. Against the backdrop of the old factories were a collection of working class neighborhoods. They weren't corrupt bureaucrats and businessmen, but they also weren't drug dealers and pimps. These were the folk who tried to earn a living honestly. The middle class might not have had as many advantages as the children of the supremely rich, but Aiden still thought he might have a better chance at accomplishing something in life if he had been born into a family that made a living wage. Aiden's father had been a garbage man… when he was able to keep a job.

The bar was certainly nicer than Bartley's place, but that wasn't saying much. A soup kitchen was a nicer place to eat than Bartley's place. The Northeastern Tavern was flooded with light and there were pleasant looking people there; pretty young college girls, business people, and young couples. Everybody was smiling, laughing, and conversing. It seemed unusual to Aiden who always associated alcohol with down-on-their-luck bums discussing their bleak prospects on life. These were not the type of folk Aiden was usually around, and that made Aiden all the more thankful.

The hostess, a thirty something woman, came up and asked Aiden where he would like to sit. She wasn't dressed in some skimpy outfit. She looked very respectable. She had short black hair and brown eyes. Her nametag notified Aiden that her name was Deirdre. It was a pretty name. He wasn't sure why he had never noticed that before. She had tried to talk to him last time he was there, but Aiden had been elusive. He smiled at her and she smiled back. It was surprising. Nobody ever smiled at Aiden except for hookers who wanted his money, and even then they had to struggle to look past his muddled mug. This woman seemed genuinely happy to see him.

"Hello."

"Will you please follow me?"

Aiden was taken to a booth in the corner of the room near the window. Deirdre gave him a menu and asked him what he would like to drink. He told her water and she left. Aiden briefly glanced at the menu. He couldn't remember when he last ate. He thought about the reporter. *How old was he? Did he have a family? Was his career promising?* Aiden shook his head. Deirdre came back with his water. She asked him what he would like to eat and he told her steak.

"It's going to rain soon."

"I walked here so that's going to be a real pain in the ass. I hope you don't have any trouble getting home."

"I have four wheel drive, it's a sturdy truck. It was my father's. He's an old redneck type. He lives out in the western part of the state."

"What does your father drive now?"

"He's retired. He doesn't even need to step outside the house much. He's very self-sufficient. He's one of those people who's always preparing for the apocalypse. Still; as paranoid as he is I sometimes have trouble arguing with him. I mean who knows if the world will end tomorrow. Then he's going to have the last laugh."

Deirdre stopped talking and left. He was happy to see her leave. A half hour later Aiden finished his meal and left the pub. His mind swirled with troubled thoughts. As he walked the gray sky gave way to storm clouds and Aiden could feel droplets of water pecking at his neck. It didn't bother him. There were far too many other things that were stressing him out. The rain started to pelt him harder. He heard lightning in the distance, and a red truck pulled over to the side of the curb. The window of the vehicle rolled down and Aiden could see Deirdre smiling at him.

"Need a ride?"

Aiden wanted to say no, but he wanted to get out of the storm even more so. Deirdre leaned over and opened the door for him. He thanked her when he got inside.

"It's a bit of a mess out there, isn't it?"

Aiden nodded, but didn't reply. His mind was still focused on other issues.

"What do you do for a living?"

"I'm a butcher."

"I grew up next to a bunch of farms. A lot of people would look down on that type of profession, but it's a really valuable career. I used to hunt all the time growing up. I'm a bit of a tomboy I guess. How long have you lived in the city?"

"My whole life."

"I just moved here. It's quite a different experience than out west. It's a nice difference though. I mean both are nice in different ways. I like the solitude and peacefulness of the country, but I like the convenience of the city. I don't remember why I eventually came to the city; I've always been adventurous. I can't tell you all the wacky stories of my growing up years..."

Aiden's mind wandered. He looked at her lips. They were moving so fast. He was amazed. *How could anybody talk that fast?* She started telling him about a squirrel she kept as a pet that used to play fetch.

"You have any wacky stories?"

Aiden wasn't sure what to say. He still hadn't absorbed everything Deirdre had said. His head was throbbing. Luckily she didn't wait for him to respond. She slapped her forehead and snorted while she attempted to suppress a laugh.

"I cannot believe I forgot to ask you where you live."

"That's okay. I live on the Southside. I can point it out to you."

Deirdre was finally calm and quiet for a while as she started to focus on the road.

"Actually this sort of works out; I live on the southern edge of the Westside so you probably don't live too far from where I do."

It wasn't long before they were back at the motel. The rain had stopped just in time, and the sun began to poke its head through the clouds.

"Look at that!"

Deirdre laughed again. Aiden gave a genuine smile, but it was closed.

"I'm sorry, but what's your name? Another thing I never asked you."

"…Aiden."

They shook hands.

"Well I hope to see you again."

"I should be back up. I really like the Tavern."

He got out of the truck and waved to Deirdre once more, but as he passed through the parking lot on the way to his room he discovered that all the panic dwelling within him had dissipated. Aiden watched the news when he got inside. He didn't know if he should. He was feeling good about himself. A rare occasion. Why spoil it by watching fear mongering exploitive news anchors talk about problems they have absolutely no idea how to solve? It might be wise to keep track of how much the public knew. The first story on tonight was about the discovery of the prosecutor's body in the river beside the park. Aiden watched the man's wife and two daughters cry and scream their anger on television. *You know you're going to hell. I* know. There was a police officer being interviewed. He explained that the culprit was probably male, black, and living in the southern part of town. Aiden decided to turn off the television; his phone rang as he did.

"Aiden? How are you doing?"

"I'm fine, Bartley. What do you want?"

"I'm just calling to give you some information on that reporter fellow. His name is Zachary Bryant. He lives alone. He's a placid man. He stays at home and works most nights. I'm sending over Quinn. He isn't going to help. I just want you to bring him along so he can watch what you do."

"I'm fine."

"Yeah, but he's already on his way."

"Wait, when is this guy coming over?"

"Well… I sent him out ten minutes ago. He's driving a black van."

Aiden got up off the bed and looked out the window. Sure enough there was a vehicle similar to the description Bartley had just given. Leaning against the vehicle was a young blonde haired youth. He didn't look much older than twenty. He had bright blue eyes, a nice looking tan suit, and his hair was neatly brushed to the left side of his head. Aiden hung up the phone and stepped outside.

The New Boy

"You must be Quinn?"

"…And you are Aiden?"

"Let's get this over with."

Aiden walked around the van. Quinn attempted to get back in the driver's seat.

"I'm driving."

Quinn didn't argue. Aiden found it odd how silent he was.

"I know you're new, but you'll have to learn fast. I'm not a babysitter."

"It'll be a while yet before I am ready."

His voice was cold and flat like a razor blade.

"Can you stop talking like that?"

"Talking like what?"

"Stop acting so calm. I never was ready to kill."

Quinn said nothing back and the ride was quiet. Aiden focused on the directions he was given. There was information on the back of the photo. He tried not to look at the front. He had memorized the address. He looked for the correct numbers on the mailboxes outside people's houses. Quinn was rapping his fingers on the dashboard.

"How you going to kill him?"

Aiden didn't reply. Instead he parked the van beside the sidewalk. They were out of the Southside. They were in the western part of the city and the old decaying factories hulked in the background. Aiden briefly glimpsed at the reporter's house. The lights were off. It was late. Aiden hadn't seen the reporter come home so perhaps he was already in bed.

"We'll stay here until the reporter goes in or comes out of that house."

Quinn nestled down in his seat and rested his face in the palm of his hand. Aiden had gone some nights without sleep, but never when he was contained in such a small space.

"Shouldn't you be awake?"

"Shut up."

Aiden's words were broken by a yawn. He looked back over at the reporter's house. The scene still looked as it had all night, but then the door knob started to turn. Aiden watched excitedly. It was over. It was really over! It didn't seem possible. The reporter stepped outside. Aiden wondered what time it was. He guessed it was close to six in the morning. The sun wasn't up, but the horizon had lightened. Orange and pink tendrils spread out across the sky.

Aiden looked at the reporter. He was a young man. He wasn't dressed fancy. He had a sweatshirt and jeans as well as a black cap on his head tilted down. A thick black beard covered the lower half of his face. He had small squinty eyes and a large hawkish nose. Quinn watched the reporter with some delight. It was the first time Aiden had seen Quinn show any sort of emotion.

"When do you think the time will be right?"

"After we've studied him longer, but I don't like killing until I'm sure it's safe."

"Did you bring a weapon?"

Aiden pointed to another man not far away who was running with his dog.

"If we pounced out and started firing like you said then we would have been seen."

"Yeah…"

"You really haven't killed anyone before? You have to think things through. You should do everything in your power to avoid death. Death always complicates things."

Quinn didn't come up with a rebuttal. He put his apathetic steel face back on and looked out the window. Aiden sighed.

"We know he gets up at five in the morning. We'll come back tonight again and see if there is a pattern that plays out."

The reporter got into his car and left. Aiden drove away from the curb.

"Quinn, I've got to get some coffee. You feel like breakfast?"

"Sure."

They went to the nearest restaurant Aiden could find.

"Ah shit, it's closed."

Aiden looked at Quinn. The boy had no emotion in his features. Aiden supposed his lack of a reaction could have been caused by a lack of sleep, but he needed to be certain.

"Before we start working more together, before we even go eat… I have to know who you are."

Quinn brushed a single hair that fell over his eye. He looked shaky. He was biting his thumb nail.

"I'll tell my story if you tell me yours."

"I'm not sure what there is to tell. I grew up in a working class family. I struggled through high school. I dropped out. My parents kicked me out of their home and Bartley took me in. What about you?"

It almost sounded like a retort. Aiden felt swallowed by fear. He didn't think a confession would be so hard. He thought he would be able to say.

"I don't have to answer you."

"You promised!"

"I'm the boss, not you."

"You got to tell me… that's not fair."

Ouroboros | 23

Quinn's defense was broken by the loud laughter coming from Aiden. He held his stomach and started to get teary eyed.

"You really think life's fair?"

"Shut up."

Aiden only laughed harder. Quinn jumped onto Aiden and put his hands around his throat. Aiden couldn't believe what was happening. He was still chuckling even as he was attacked. Aiden started to punch Quinn in the face frantically. He could feel himself losing oxygen. His eyes were bulging out of his head. His punches did little to save him. He could see fury in Quinn's eyes. He really intended to kill him. Well... maybe not kill him. He knew Quinn had a lot of rage. Aiden stopped trying to hit Quinn. It was a difficult task. Aiden was in panic mode. He couldn't breathe. He had seen this behavior in a number of his victims. People lose control when they are afraid, but he couldn't do that now. He unlocked the door instead.

The two men fell out of the vehicle and into the snowy parking lot. Quinn no longer had as firm of a grasp on Aiden. Aiden pulled Quinn close. He reversed their positions. Aiden pinned Quinn down with his knee. He began to pummel Quinn striking his face again and again with more force every time his fist came down. Aiden knew he had to stop. Quinn was lying on the gravel with his eyes closed, but he was breathing. A back tooth had been knocked out in the brawl. Blood dripped down his chin. The bottom lobe of his left ear was split. *He's starting to look like you.* Aiden was breathing heavily. There still wasn't anybody in the parking lot. It was still dark out. Aiden knew it would be a while before the sun came up. Aiden grabbed Quinn and hauled him back to the passenger's seat of the van.

"What the hell am I going to do with you?"

Aiden leaned up against the van and stood for a moment in order to clear his head. He had to think. He would have to come up with a solution quickly because Aiden knew Quinn could awake at any time. Aiden walked around the van and decided to drive back to the motel. He drove in silence. Occasionally he peered over to check on Quinn, but there didn't seem to be anything to worry about. Aiden discovered Quinn wasn't all that much of an expert on fighting and the only reason he managed to get on top of Aiden first was because he launched a surprise attack, but that failed, and now Aiden was on edge, but he was too tired to think about any of this. Aiden started to drift out of his lane.

"Oh shit!"

He nearly sideswiped another car. The opposing vehicle honked, and the driver flipped Aiden off as he passed. Aiden shook his head. They would be back at the motel any minute now. All he had to do was make a couple of turns. Aiden saw the girls were still out. He couldn't imagine they would still be working much longer. Their shift ended when the sun came up. Aiden parked near his motel room, and carried Quinn by putting Quinn's arm around his neck. One of the girls looked at Aiden funny. She was in high heels and wore fishnet stocking. She had big looped earrings and a lot of make-up. She was chewing bubble gum.

"What's up with your pal their honey?"

"A little too many drinks."

The girl shrugged and turned her attention to another man who was offering her a handful of cash. Aiden threw Quinn down on his bed, and shut the door. Aiden went to the bathroom to wash his face. There was a mini-fridge next to Aiden's bed. He walked over to it and pulled out a bottle of water. He began to pour the contents over Quinn's face. He sputtered and coughed before sitting up and breathing heavily. He looked confused until he saw Aiden, and then he began to scowl.

"Why the hell did you bring me here?"

"You're lucky I didn't kill you."

Aiden was blatant and suddenly Quinn's features softened. He looked genuinely horrified.

"I'm so sorry. I don't know what I was thinking."

Aiden went into the bathroom and sat on the toilet. He kept the bathroom door open so he could still see Quinn.

"Well… let's talk about it."

"I've always wanted respect. I met Bartley and he offered me a job as a busboy. I knew what he did. It seemed exciting so I asked Bartley if I could be a foot soldier. He refused, but I kept asking, and he eventually relented."

"You tried to strangle me because you were offended?"

"You were laughing at me. I wanted respect. Nobody has ever given me any gratitude for the things I've accomplished."

Aiden started laughing hard. He bent over and he looked up at Quinn with tears in his eyes. Quinn's face grew red, but Aiden slapped his knee.

"Who the hell do you think you are?"

Quinn was biting his lip tenaciously until he drew blood. Quinn started to get off the couch. Aiden was still laughing, but he pointed a finger at Quinn.

"You sit right there, you're going to be laughed at and there won't be a thing you'll do about it."

Quinn sat back on the bed. He didn't look happy, but he didn't argue.

"That's a good boy. I'm going to avoid saying anything that might upset you, but only if you're not going to have any more outbursts. Understand?"

Quinn shook his head still staring at Aiden darkly.

"You're going to leave and don't come back until eight or nine. I want some rest."

Quinn got off the bed like he was ordered and stormed out of the room. Aiden crawled onto the bed when he heard the door slam, and put his hands under his head. He looked up at the ceiling for a moment. He wondered how difficult it would be to kill the reporter. Aiden had several pistols under his mattress that he could use. He bought his weapons from a friend of Bartley's.

Aiden drifted into his subconscious. His dream that night was of him drowning. It wasn't an unusual dream or his most terrifying, but he didn't know where he was. In a lake. In the ocean. All he knew was that the water was deep and he couldn't breathe. He was sinking and it was growing darker. Aiden could see a circle of white light above him. Above the water. Aiden didn't know what it was. Was it the sun? The light grew dimmer and dimmer the deeper Aiden went until there was no light at all. He was surrounded by blackness.

Aiden awoke in a cold sweat. He had thrown off the thin blanket covering him. He grabbed his chest. Aiden never thought about heart problems. He wasn't overweight. Aiden hadn't been to a doctor in over a decade. He didn't figure there was any point. Aiden didn't intend on living to a ripe old age. Most likely he would get shot dead on one of his jobs. He took his hand away. He looked at Ouroboros. Aiden's phone started to ring. Aiden picked it up.

"Hello?"

Silence.

"Aiden?"

It was his father.

"Why are you calling? You know I'm not going to come over."

"I know. I just. I wanted to hear you again. The doctors say…"

"Do you really think I care?"

Aiden hung up. It had become unbearable. His anger bubbled up like water in a heated pot. He didn't know what would happen if he stayed on the line. Aiden checked the time on his phone. His father had called before. Aiden thought the conversation was pointless. Aiden hadn't spoken with the old man in over a month. He hadn't seen him in three years. Aiden yawned. He tried to forget about the phone call. Aiden had slept all day. It was seven o' clock. Aiden thought about the reporter. Quinn would be coming back soon.

Wednesday, January 17th, 58 days left

Aiden washed his face. He took a couple of pain killers, the last in the bottle. *Damn... where did they all go?* Aiden heard his phone ring. He was afraid to answer it. Would it be his father again? He walked over and picked it up, but it was Bartley.

"How your trip with Quinn go?"

"Like hell, he tried to kill me!"

"You can't be serious?"

"Jesus Christ. He tried to strangle me."

"Alright, alright. Send him back. I'll deal with him."

"No, don't hurt him. I'll keep him. I think I've worked things over."

Aiden heard a car door shut, he walked over to the window of his motel room and looked through the blinds.

"He's here anyway."

Aiden hung up before Bartley said goodbye. He went to open the door. He grabbed a pistol from under his mattress. He opened the door. Quinn was glaring at him, but then looked down at the gun Aiden was holding.

"You going to use that?"

There was a quiver in his voice. Aiden didn't answer right away. He looked down at the pistol as if it just occurred to him he was holding a weapon.

"Yes, but not on you."

Aiden walked outside. Quinn followed and shut the door behind him.

"Who's car we taking?"

"Yours is a little less conspicuous."

"So this going to be all night?"

Aiden nodded and Quinn sighed. Aiden put the key into the ignition.

"Where did you go after I kicked you out?"

"Back to my place."

Aiden started to drive out of the parking lot.

"Where's that?"

"You're not going shoot to me in my sleep?"

"If I was going to kill you I would have done it already and I usually don't kill people while they are sleeping."

Aiden continued to drive without further conversation. They reached the reporter's house and he parked a block away.

"What are you doing?"

"I think it would be suspicious if a black van that doesn't belong to either of the neighbors parked in the same place a second day in a row."

Aiden and Quinn waited. They both knew it would be for a long time. The sun went down completely. It grew very dark. Aiden never saw the reporter come home. He must get home early. Aiden looked over to see Quinn was asleep. Aiden nudged him on the arm and Quinn groaned like a child being stirred from a nap.

"How much longer?"

"Four more hours."

Aiden looked at the time on his phone. It was two in the morning. Aiden could feel the heaviness of his lids. He slapped himself and then he slapped Quinn.

"Hey! I was awake."

"Yeah, but I just felt like hitting you."

The two managed to stay awake until the sun rose. Cars had come intermittently through the night, but they came more frequently as the sun rose higher in the sky.

"Hey... Quinn! There he is!"

Aiden pointed to the reporter who was coming out of his house. He still wasn't dressed yet. He wore a wife beater and some shorts, but not much else. He didn't wear any shoes. Just long black socks that were tall enough to reach his knees.

"I want you to drive around the block."

"You're doing it now?"

"Waiting too long is as bad as attacking too soon."

Quinn started driving as soon as Aiden was out. Aiden held the revolver behind his back. He walked stiffly, but he hoped he wouldn't seem too strange. He was within a hundred feet of the reporter. The man must have realized something was off about Aiden, but he didn't realize it soon enough.

"What seems to be the problem?"

Aiden revealed his revolver. The reporter's eyes widened. He froze like a deer in headlights. The flight or fight response sometimes takes a while to kick in. People aren't animals. They aren't used to danger on a regular basis. Not northern folk anyway. Aiden squeezed the trigger. The blast of a gun is louder than most people expect. Aiden had gotten used to it. In the beginning of his career he had worn ear protection, but he didn't care anymore about the ringing sound in his ears. The reporter fell. He had been hit three times in the chest at close range, but he was still breathing. People die slow. You had to hit them in the perfect spot to kill them right away.

The man tried crawling back to his home, leaving a trail of blood behind him. He tried calling for help. He was on his stomach when Aiden fired the last three rounds into the man's back. The man stopped moving. He was still breathing, but his breathing slowed. Aiden looked around for witnesses. He saw the black van was pulling around. Quinn had opened the door. Aiden climbed inside while the van was still moving. Quinn tried to race off from the scene as soon as Aiden shut the door.

"Slow down."

Quinn nodded and checked his speed. Aiden began wiping down his revolver with a cloth from his pocket.

"What do we do?"

Quinn was shaking, but Aiden remained calm.

"Just keep driving. Go back to the motel."

Quinn started scratching the back of his neck. He looked all over.

"What are you looking for?"

"Police lights."

He said it loudly as if the answer were obvious, but Aiden gave a short smug laugh.

"What?"

Quinn turned his head sharply at Aiden. Aiden was still looking down cleaning his revolver.

"Calm yourself and keep your eyes on the road. You don't have to worry about the police. Bartley's got men in the force. They'll keep our tails clean."

Quinn looked skeptical, but he didn't argue. They got back to the motel shortly before ten. They waited in the car. They were both quiet. Aiden rested his head back. His eyes dropped low. He wasn't asleep. He was thinking. When did he last eat? Did he have anything back in the motel? He turned his head to Quinn to tell him he was going inside. Quinn's hands were still clutching the steering wheel tightly. He was looking out his window back and forth. Sweat was still pouring down his face.

"It'll get better kid. Everybody's nervous their first time. You got smart people looking out for you. Bartley's good at his work. He's a scumbag... but he's smart. Just get something to drink."

Quinn looked back at Aiden. His short quick breaths extended and his chest wasn't moving up and down so quickly. Quinn swallowed.

"Who was the first person you killed?"

"Vladimir Kaminski. Half the Russians you'll ever meet are named Vladimir or Viktor. They love the V's."

"Did you get drunk the first time?"

Aiden shook his head.

"I don't drink."

"Oh."

"I slept for a long time... I strangled him in his own home. I broke in late at night. I watched him for a while as he slept. He was snoring so loudly."

Aiden chuckled. Then he went back to cleaning his revolver. The gun didn't need to be cleaned anymore.

"Did you shoot him?"

"I could have shot him. It would have been quicker. I could have done anything. I thought I was so cool. I had a wire in my hands. I felt like a ninja. I was dressed in black. Sleek like James Bond. I wrapped the wire around his throat. He woke up. He started jerking around. He kicked and tried to head-butt me. He was an older man, as old as I am now. I was still in my twenties. I was able to… It took thirty minutes for him to die."

Aiden shook his head. As if he was disagreeing with himself. He stuffed his revolver back into his pants.

"It really took that long?"

"People cling to life so tightly. It's admirable. It really is. People like us, who take it away? I don't know. I've known very few members of my profession. I don't talk to many people. I get the job over with as quickly as possible. I go home and I sleep."

"You think it'll ever get better?"

Aiden looked at him. He noticed Quinn had the brightest blue eyes he had ever seen. He looked so young.

"No… Go home and don't leave your home unless you have to."

Aiden shut his door as he got out. He heard Quinn start the engine and drive off. He didn't say goodbye. Every ounce of energy he had was being used to put one foot in front of the other. When he got to his room he collapsed on the bed. He groaned when he realized that he should probably take a bath. When did he have one last, and did he *really* need it? He was so tired. He smelled himself. Yep, he needed one.

He threw himself back on his feet. He turned on the water and sat on the toilet. He rubbed his face. Aiden undressed and slipped into the water. It was colder than he would have liked, but eventually his body warmed up to the temperature. He was starting to relax. He felt good. Still tired, but calm until his phone rang. Aiden's headache returned. Aiden leaned over the tub. His wet arm dripped over the floor. He grabbed his pants and reached into his pocket. He checked the number. It was his father. Aiden's heart started to pound itself against his rib cage. Aiden felt short of breath. Why was he so afraid?

"Hello?"

"… I want you to come over. Please don't ask me why. Can you just do it? My health is getting worse. I'm not going to defend what I did. Come here and curse me out. I can take that…"

Aiden was so sure he was going to say no. Not just sure, that's what he expected to come out of his mouth, but for whatever reason what came out was, "when?"

Aiden couldn't believe what he had just said. That couldn't have been him that had spoken those words. It must have been somebody else, but who? Why did Aiden just do that? His father was quiet. Aiden wasn't sure what his father was thinking either. How could he have guessed that Aiden would say what he said? There was a long pause.

"Hello?"

"I'm sorry, the old man said, I didn't think… I am beyond overjoyed by your response… It's simply taking me a while to process."

Aiden gave the old man a short time to collect himself.

"Yes… of course. You can come over anytime. It's really up to you."

"I'll be over when I'm over."

He thought he heard his father say thank you before he hung up. Aiden finished washing himself, and then he dried himself with a towel hanging up on the back of the door. He changed into some clean clothes, although his supply on laundry that wasn't dirty was running low. He knew he would have to go to the laundromat soon. Aiden collapsed on his bed and quickly fell asleep. He didn't wake again until the middle of the afternoon the next morning day with a raging headache. He groaned and turned sideways only to ungracefully fall on the floor. Aiden groaned some more.

He thought about where he should go. He knew at some point he would have to make a stop at Bartley's to collect his money. He wasn't sure where else from there. That bar up on the north side was nice. *With the woman. What was her name? Oh yeah... Deirdre. She seemed really interesting.* He realized for the first time in the longest time he was excited about the future.

Thursday, January 18th, 57 days left

Aiden wanted to be cautious. He would go to Bartley's bar first. That seemed like an okay place to be, but from there he would force himself north and maybe even talk to the woman at the bar. It was evening by the time he left. He would drive the station wagon. He didn't like driving and he usually didn't have to. Everyplace he wanted to go was within walking distance, but today he felt tired. He had been sleeping too much. He read in an article once that the more you sleep the more tired you became. It must have been true because Aiden slept all the time. He got into his car which was a mess. The back seat was impenetrable. Garbage, books and left over food was strewn everywhere. It was like the inside of his motel room.

He started up the engine which sputtered and coughed before evening out. He pulled out of the parking lot and started to drive to Bartley's bar. Aiden arrived at the bar and parked a block away. It looked busy tonight. Aiden pulled his usual stunt. He cut in front of the crowd and was let in by Mike the bouncer. Bartley sat in the corner listening to a performer with several other associates. It seemed like an identical scene compared to the last time except there wasn't a band, just a single man playing the harmonica and singing the blues.

The associates were different too. There was only one police officer this time. The man Aiden had seen on the news talking about the murder of the prosecutor. The police officer and Bartley were whispering to each other and laughing like a young couple out on a date. Aiden smiled inside his head. Quinn was also at the table looking very fashionable. He was dressed in a stylish black suit. He was leaning back in his chair looking very comfortable, but he seemed to be distracted by some distant thought. A lost look was in his eyes. He was in his own world. The third man was a Black with a tattoo that signified he belonged to a local gang. One Bartley had allied with. A skull with three lines slashed diagonally to the left across the skull's face. Aiden sat between the Black and Quinn.

"Do you have my money?"

Bartley; the pudgy little dwarf; looked at Aiden with his face resting in the palm of his hand.

"Am I having Déjà vu?"

Aiden didn't respond. He stared at Bartley for a while until Bartley sighed and threw across an envelope full of money. Aiden checked carefully what he had received.

"I need pain killers."

Bartley looked at him strangely.

"You're out already? That was supposed to last you a month."

"Just give me what I need."

"Fine."

He looked behind himself at a man sitting on the other side of the bar. When the two men caught each other's eyes the man Bartley was looking at got up and started walking over. The man reached into his pocket and pulled out a prescription bottle. He threw it to Bartley and Bartley threw it to Aiden. Aiden put the bottle in his pocket.

"Do you have a job you want me to do or can I leave?"

"You're free to leave anytime you want."

Aiden sighed and left. It started to snow just as his fingers curled around the handle of the car door. He looked up at the sky which was a pale color. A snowflake landed on his cheek and melted. It would be February soon and Christmas was long over. The time when the city would dress itself in colorful lights and everybody would be a little nicer to each other. Christmas meant nothing for Aiden. He didn't believe in anything, and he didn't have anybody to celebrate the holidays with. He remembered being excited at Christmas time. He'd sneak downstairs and try to catch a glimpse of Santa Clause only to find his father passed out drunk on the couch.

Aiden decided that he would go to the bar on the North side. He wasn't sure why. It wasn't just because of the woman, but he had the strongest suspicion that if he went back to the motel then he would kill himself. Aiden started driving. He turned on the radio. The news was on; a story about the dead reporter. The news lady started talking about his life and how he did everything to make the city a better place to live. She was turning him into a martyr. Aiden thought it was funny. Nobody cared about the man until he died, but now everyone is talking about him. Aiden never understood martyrs. He thought they were annoying. People will look for any way to immortalize themselves. Aiden hoped to be forgotten. He would give anything if people simply never remembered him ever again. He swallowed a pill. It was time to see that woman.

Snow was coming down faster. The radio said a blizzard would come tomorrow. It was no secret that Aiden loved the snow. He loved the cold. Aiden loved the silence after snow had come. Even in the city things were quieter. Like God had hushed the world. Aiden was able to calm himself. Things are getting better. *Someday you will make up for the harm you've done.* Aiden didn't believe it. *I'm pretty sure I'm going to decompose in a wet gutter,* another thought retorted. Aiden got to the bar and the snow had already piled up about three inches. It was a thick snow too. It would be a long time before it melted away. He would have to get a new coat. His old windbreaker just wasn't going to cut it anymore. Those were problems for another day. He had a chance to meet the woman in the bar. She looked nice. Aiden was curious to see her again.

Aiden smelled his breath. It wasn't as sour as it usually was. He brushed his thick black hair back. It was tangled and matted, but good enough. That seemed to be the epitome of Aiden's physical features. Good enough. Aiden walked inside the bar. A girl; not Deirdre, asked Aiden if he would like to be seated at a booth or on a stool. Aiden told her a booth. He was taken to a shadowy corner of the bar. Then the girl asked what Aiden would like to drink. He told her water. *This will go good. Don't be alarmed. Don't panic.* Aiden was hunkered low over the table staring out the window. A man and a woman sitting not far away gave worried looks. They saw Aiden and asked for the bill. *Everything I do crumbles to dust and flows out of my fingers,* Aiden thought. *It'll be alright,* a different thought comforted him. The young waitress came over and delivered Aiden his drink.

"Would you like something to eat?"

"A… steak… Do you know a woman named Deidre? Do you know where she lives?"

"I'm sorry sir. I couldn't tell you."

Aiden nodded and the girl left. *I knew it wouldn't work.* He sat forlorn for the next hour, and even when his steak arrived he decided he wasn't hungry. Aiden paid the bill. He rubbed his face and walked back into the parking lot of the bar ready to leave.

"Hey wait… Aiden?"

Aiden was about to open his car door, but he turned around. A thin woman with a pale face and black hair stood in the snow. A cold wave of wind bashed against her face. She brushed one long dark tendril out of her eye. She smiled at Aiden. He gave a closed smile back.

"What are you doing here?"

"I wanted to see you again."

Deirdre was bundled up in a thick winter coat that was too big for her. She looked like she was lost in the massive expanse of fabric. She walked over to him.

"I just got off a couple of hours ago. I came back to get reading glasses, I left them in the kitchen."

Aiden nodded then looked around.

"You want to get something to eat ...not here."

Deirdre laughed. Aiden liked her laugh, he wasn't sure why, but he smiled with her. It was a closed smile.

"Sure. I know a great place. You want to follow me or actually you can come in my car. I don't want you to waste any gas."

Aiden followed Deirdre. He liked looking at her. She seemed more beautiful than last time. He didn't know why. They came to her vehicle. Aiden slid in the front of Deirdre's red truck while she pulled out of the parking lot.

"My car's a mess."

"The station wagon? It's not that bad. Listen. Everyone goes through financial struggles. I may have a job, but believe me I had to struggle just like everyone else when the economy went bad."

Not *just* like everyone else. Was she attracted to him? Aiden couldn't figure it out. What possible worth could he have to a girl like her?

"So... what do you like to do?"

Deirdre looked up again. He remained patiently quiet and waited for her to talk.

"I like pottery and painting."

"I don't really know much about art."

"Surely you like to be creative sometimes though? I mean… art is what distinguishes us from animals along with our ability to reason and show compassion."

Aiden looked out the window. The moonlight reflected off the snow. It was as bright as day.

"I guess I'm not human."

Aiden's voice was low. Deirdre smiled and rolled her eyes thinking Aiden had been joking.

"Well then tell me what you do. What do you enjoy? I hope it's not butchering animals."

Aiden was almost tempted to say yes. He tried to think. What did he enjoy? I like going for walks. I like being alone. *You have all the likability of a serial killer. Can't you be more engaging?* Aiden shook himself.

"What was that?"

"I'm sorry it's a nervous tick. I'm weird like that."

"No you're not; you just got a few problems. Everyone's got their problems."

Keep calm. You've got nothing to worry about. He stayed motionless for a second. He felt sick. He was so used to shaking himself to get rid of bad thoughts, but eventually the pain in his gut subsided. He laughed out loud. He didn't mean to.

"I'm sorry. I just… I don't know what to say. I didn't shake. I was just about to, but I didn't."

Deirdre was smiling with him. She was giving Aiden another funny look. She was staring at his mouth. Aiden grew red and he put his lips back together.

"Sorry."

"You worry too much. Just tell me what happened."

"I got into a lot of fights when I was younger."

Deirdre was quiet for a long time. She eventually pulled into the parking lot of a family diner. She was about to get out of the car, but Aiden grabbed her wrist.

"Hey? What are you doing?"

Aiden let go. He put his head down like a dog who had been scolded.

"I'm sorry. I just need to know. Why are you doing all of this? I'm such a mess. Why are you going out with me?"

He looked at Deirdre, but she put her head down.

"I lied to you. My father isn't retired. He's in prison."

"What'd he do?"

Deirdre didn't respond. Aiden didn't think she was ever going to respond. It seemed like the two of them would be sitting in that red truck for eternity.

"He shot a man at a convenience store and stole the money. He got caught not much longer after that. The man he shot died. Dad got a life sentence. I was raised by mom till I was old enough to leave. She... well I don't want talk too much about what she did."

Aiden could see her trembling. He moved his hand closer to her.

"Don't!"

Aiden recoiled. Deirdre had a cold callus stare that penetrated Aiden. Her features softened and she looked guilty again. She put her head down.

"I'm sorry. I've cried as much as I'm ever going to in this life. I just can't bring myself to break down again. Don't know what might happen If I did. Just please... let me be. Why I like you? I guess because we're not too different."

More silence. Aiden and Deirdre looked away and out their windows. It had started to snow. After a while Deirdre said, "Let's go inside."

"I don't think I've ever been to this place," Aiden said when they approached the entrance, "The city is always changing. I know a lot of conservative types don't like that, but I find it refreshing. Maybe it's because I feel like the sooner I forget the past the better."

Deirdre gave a subtle smile. Aiden gave a closed smile back. The restaurant was small. A few booths and a couple of tables were all that Aiden could see. There were some stools too, but he figured the place could seat at most maybe twenty-five people at one time. There was a sign that said seat yourself. Aiden let Deirdre choose.

"You don't have to be so chivalrous."

"I wasn't *being* polite. I just don't know where I want to sit."

Deirdre picked a table in the back corner of the room. She was still quiet.

"Hey listen... I got to tell you some things about me," Aiden tried to say, but before he could finish a waitress came over and placed two glasses of water down. She seemed very perky. Completely unaware of the moodiness of her two patrons.

"What can I get you to drink?"

Her voice was bubbly. Aiden rubbed his forehead.

"Water is fine."

He didn't even look up at his server.

"I need something to drink... wine."

Deirdre looked at Aiden with a smile.

"What were you going to tell me?"

The waitress was gone. Aiden's mouth felt dry. His heart beat quickly. Sweat emerged from his pores. He could be calm when he killed. He was used to that.

"I'm a crook, Deirdre."

He tried to keep his voice low, but he threw the words out there as fast as he could. He couldn't contain himself. She had to know.

"What?"

"I'm a crook, I work for the mob."

"You can't be serious."

"Look at me. What else could I be doing?"

It took a moment for Deirdre to realize what she was being told. She started to scowl. Deirdre picked up her water and splashed it on Aiden.

"What the fuck is wrong with you?"

Her tone was seething. She started to leave. Aiden was frozen. What had he done? He wiped his dripping face with a napkin and brushed his hair back. He got up from the table and tried to chase Deirdre down.

"Sir?"

The waitress stood in front of Aiden as he started to leave. Aiden tried to explain himself.

"It's a, I mean… here."

Aiden ran back and put a ten dollar bill on the table before running outside. Deirdre was trying to get into her car. Deidre put her finger up when she saw him.

"You stay away from me, Aiden."

He stopped walking. It was snowing heavily. Aiden put his hands up like he had a gun pointed at him.

"Deirdre…You need to hear me out."

Deirdre kept shaking her head back and forth. She was pacing and had her arms wrapped around herself. Puffs of cold air gathered around her mouth.

"I'm a crook. It's true. I'm so much worse than that. You must have seen something in me though. I don't do the things I do because I want to do them. I do them because it's the only thing I know. I keep thinking things will get better, but they never do."

Deirdre looked up at him. She didn't look angry. She looked empathetic. Aiden thought he had got her, but Deirdre shut her eyes and pulled her hair.

"NO!"

Her yell resonated and echoed all around them. She fell to her knees.

"I can't do this anymore. I can't trust someone who just lies all the time. Who keeps telling me things will get better…"

Her arms were wrapped around herself. She was crying unrestrained. The tears flowed from her face. She kept trying to wipe them away, but they were persistent.

"Things will get better. You have to try."

Aiden took one hesitant step forward. He kneeled down next to Deirdre and put his arms around her. He pressed her head against his chest. Her nails dug into his skin. She continued to sob. Aiden found himself crying with her. Tears flowing freely down his face. He put his chin on top of her head and hugged Deidre even tighter. Then after her cries had lessened she started to pull away.

"Get off… Get OFF!"

She pushed Aiden so forcefully that he banged his head against the car parked next to Deirdre's truck. She sighed as she stood up. Aiden rubbed the sore bump on his head and stood up too.

"You okay?"

Aiden nodded.

"I'm going to leave now."

Aiden coughed awkwardly. She looked at him.

"What?"

"It's just that you brought me here."

Deirdre slapped her forehead and gave a small laugh. She wiped her eyes. She leaned against her truck.

"I'm sorry Aiden… I completely forgot."

"Eh, it's okay."

"You aren't going to rob me are you?"

"I don't do that."

"I have to know what you do."

Aiden started to sweat. He wasn't sure what the right thing to say was. He didn't want to lie to her, but on the other hand he just couldn't bring himself to say he killed people. Aiden coughed.

"I'm sorry I have a sore throat. I'm not sure I can talk much more."

"Are you really trying to fool me with that?"

"Do you really want to know?"

He thought the truth would be like a band-aide. Maybe if he was quick enough it wouldn't hurt. Deirdre looked at Aiden up and down.

"Actually, just keep to yourself."

Aiden stopped sweating. He felt like he had been holding his breath for hours. The rest of the drive was quiet. Deirdre didn't even turn on the radio. The snow continued to fall. Aiden thought it looked peaceful outside. Aiden wanted to talk some more. He had never been so desperate to have a conversation, but he refrained. He knew talking would ruin the moment.

"I think you can get out now."

Deirdre parked the car next to Aiden's beat up station wagon. Aiden was about to leave the car when Deirdre grabbed his wrist. Aiden turned around.

"I'd like to see you again."

"Me too."

He wondered if what he said made sense.

"I mean I want to see you again... Not me. My ego's not that huge. I know I'm pretty great, but still..."

Deirdre pulled him back down and kissed him.

"You talk too much."

She let him go. Aiden wanted to say something clever. He wanted this moment to last forever. He wanted to say something perfect. Instead he stuttered, said some gibberish, and then straightened himself out.

"I guess I'll see you again sometime."

Deirdre smiled and nodded. Aiden shut the door and watched as she drove away. The snow was still coming down on his shoulders. Aiden drove back to the motel in harmony with himself. It was the first time he could remember feeling so happy in forever. He was still skeptical. *Let's not ruin everything, there is still more that has to be done.* He even considered a visit to his father's. He felt nauseous even thinking about it, but he did make a promise even if that promise was something he desperately wished to take back. Aiden wanted to leave all his memories behind him. *You need to see him,* he thought. No, Aiden responded aloud. *You need to go see him.* Aiden started grinding his teeth. He stopped resisting. *Could I have first a night's rest?* Aiden waited. *Are you actually going to go?* Yes.

Friday, January 19th 56 days left

Aiden had grown up on the Southside. His old neighborhood had actually gotten worse. He couldn't believe it. He hadn't been down this street in a decade. Everything was a dilapidated version of its old self, and its old self was already run down. Aiden recognized one building... the old library. Its roof had caved in and one side had partially sunk into the ground. Vines entangled the building and it seemed as if the earth itself were trying to swallow the structure whole. The windows were all busted and the paint had long since chipped away. *Damn. What happened to you?* Snow began to fall through the gaping hole.

Not all his memories were terrible. Good ones existed, but they were lost in a sea of awful events. For every one good moment Aiden could recount he could pick three or four bad ones. He saw the house of his first girlfriend. He smiled. Then as he drove he saw the alleyway where some neighborhood kids beat him up. He stopped smiling. He saw the store where he had gotten caught shoplifting. He saw the telephone pole where he crashed his bike and broke his leg. It wasn't his father who had taken him to the hospital. His father was home passed out. It was instead the mother of a friend.

It made Aiden think even more about what he was doing. Did he really want to go through with this? Aiden had slept deep into the morning waking near noon. The voice inside urged him to get up and go. Aiden resisted. The voice was persistent. Aiden knew he could turn around at any point, but he didn't. He kept going, and it wasn't because of his father. This is going to end badly. THIS IS GOING TO END BADLY. THIS IS GOING TO END BADLY! A voice inside him chanted. Aiden gripped his steering wheel. He didn't shake himself. He thought about Deirdre. He felt relief. The pain subsided. Aiden made it. It was his old home.

The porch was cluttered and dusty. The lawn was all dirt. No grass. Not even weeds survived. Aiden knew it was in the late of winter, but it didn't make a difference. It could be springtime and there still wouldn't be anything. His father was lazy. After his mother died he poisoned the grass so he wouldn't have to do anything. His father wasn't out of shape. He had a beer gut, but he wasn't morbidly obese. In fact his father used to be an intimidating figure. He had thick side burns that wrapped together under his chin like the strings of a bonnet. His father never had much hair on the top of his head. All his hair seemed to be in more unusual places like the thick carpet of fur on his massive arms. He had a thick hairy chest too.

Aiden parked his car next to the curb. He didn't see any other cars nearby. When he was growing up his father drove a 1973 Ford Mustang. It was his most prized possession, but even that he didn't take care of. He got drunk and drove it into a lake. He nearly drowned and would have if it wasn't for the bystanders who called the police. The rest of the year Aiden's life got progressively worse. He was both ostracized and persecuted daily. He wasn't talked to except when somebody was mentioning an embarrassing incident. His first girlfriend; who he really didn't consider a girlfriend, dated him out of pity. Aiden got out of the car and started to walk up to the door. He gulped as his hand neared the knob. Then before he could open it the door was opened for him. Instead of seeing his father, he saw a decrepit old man in a wheel chair with an oxygen mask strapped around his face.

"Dad?"

"Come... in"

He spoke in between the repetitive noises of his respirator. Aiden followed him inside, and found that the inside of his house was even worse than outside. There were stacks of junk as tall as Aiden. Broken chairs, piles of newspapers, and DVD's were thrown together. Aiden had thought his motel was an ugly place to live. The man in the wheel chair eventually stopped in the only small amount of space available. Next to him were a table and an old corded phone.

"So this is the shit hole you've been wallowing in since I've been gone?"

The old man didn't respond. He stared at Aiden for a long time.

"You've grown... old."

"Guess that's what happens when you grow up alone."

The old man leaned over and picked up something off the ground next to the table. It was a half-finished bottle of whiskey. Aiden started to laugh.

"You can't be serious? You're really going to drink in front of me?"

Instead of drinking from the bottle, the old man started to spill the drink on the floor. Aiden hadn't been expecting this. He stepped back in surprise. The liquid almost spilled over on his shoes.

"What the hell...?"

"I haven't had a sip in three years."

"If you've changed so much then why is your house such a mess? Why are you dying in your own filth; do you have any shred of human dignity?"

"I don't think there's anything I... could have done. You still would have picked me... apart. It took everything... I had to stop drinking. I figured maybe... you could forgive me."

"You figured wrong."

"What the hell did...? I do? I know. I... I know what *I* did, but... I embarrassed you. There has to... be something... decent I've done something to... You really can't find anything right with me?"

Aiden wished he could freeze time. He wished time could stay frozen forever. He always feared what would happen next in his life that could make his existence even more unbearable. Now was one of those times. Aiden wished his father would fade away.

"You know what. I'm done here."

"Do you remember the... the day... your mother died? Do you remember what... she told you?"

"How dare you bring her into this!"

"... She told you it's all right to go on. There would be a lot... of pain...a lot of pain... but it would pass. To...To...Move on? I don't...I don't... think I can do that."

"Good. Then go ahead and die already!"

Aiden continued to leave. He didn't stop or look back until he reached his car. When he got into the station wagon he sat in silence. His mother. Aiden started to pound the steering wheel. He tried to calm down. He inhaled deeply. He put his seat belt on and started to drive. Nothing had brought him more relief in his life than seeing his home in his rear view mirror. He had no idea where he wanted to go. He could see Deidre again, but he didn't want to rush things. He wanted to take his time with her. He wanted to do something radical something he hadn't done in a long time.

Aiden drove by a church. *You can't be serious.* Yet Aiden was very serious. He figured going to church might be as hard as or even harder than visiting his father. He had a lot to answer for. The church was protestant. He didn't check the denomination. He didn't plan on staying very long. The parking lot was vacant except for a couple vehicles besides Aiden's. It was a Tuesday. He wondered who was even here. Aiden got out of the car and kept walking. It was a struggle. He reached the door, he knocked, and he waited for a few minutes. He was about to leave, but then he heard footsteps coming from inside. An old man dressed in long flowing robes answered the door. He was fat with an egg shaped head and a couple of hairs lingering on his scalp.

"May I help you?"

"I should really come back on a Sunday. I know that. I guess I was here and... I haven't believed in anything in over a decade. I guess I'm starting to see a little bit of hope in my life that I had thought was gone forever."

The minister rolled up his sleeve and looked at his watch.

"I do have to be somewhere in an hour. Duties of the church include visiting the sick and dying, but if you come in we can talk for a little while."

Aiden followed the pastor inside the cavernous old church.

"I'm sorry, but I didn't catch your name."

"My name's Aiden."

"My name's Richard Perch if you didn't see it on the sign out front."

Aiden laughed.

"What?"

"I didn't even stop to see what denomination this is."

"We're Methodist."

They continued walking until they reached a room of vast expanse. Aiden looked up at the ceiling only to be awed by its height. It looked so much larger than it did outside. Aiden and Richard sat down in a back pew.

"So, why do you no longer believe?"

Aiden took a deep breath. He wasn't sure if he was prepared to give an answer. He obviously couldn't tell the minister everything. He knew he couldn't tell him he had killed people. That was one sin nobody could forgive.

"When I was twelve I really started to question the existence of God. It wasn't because my life was awful. I questioned a lot of things growing up. I never really trusted anything anybody told me. I'm just a skeptic by nature. I guess after I learned Santa Clause wasn't real then it wasn't long before I thought God was fictional too."

"You know there is a major difference between God and mythology?"

Aiden didn't like his tone. He found it condescending, but he continued.

"I got older and I became more doubtful that there was anything after death. My life went into a tailspin. I dropped out of high school. I worked for many years working minimum wage jobs and I lived in the worst rundown homes you could imagine, but don't think for a second I stopped believing in God because my life turned sour. I'm not the type that blames my problems on anyone much less an imaginary entity."

"You sound angry."

"I'm sorry…"

Richard picked up a Bible lying next to him. He opened it up.

"Have you ever heard the story of Job?"

"God tortures a man to prove a point to the Devil. I never really liked that story."

"I read the bible like I'm reading poetry. Many of these stories are open for interpretation. The men who wrote this book were of their time and trying to understand God in the only way they knew how."

"What's your point?"

"I'm telling you not to take the Bible literally. When I read Job I see a man whose life was torn apart, but he continued to do good. That's what I take from these stories. They are parables."

"Like fairy tales?"

"Not exactly, I do think that these stories are based on fact. I don't believe they were just made up, but they could have been exaggerated. The point I'm trying to make is… do some good. Go out and try to be nice to other people. The advice I'm giving you isn't coming from a minister. It's coming from a fellow human being. If you're good to other people then your life will get better."

"Are you trying to sell me on Karma?"

"I don't think its Karma. I just think if you're nicer to other people than they'll be nicer to you… I think it's time for me to go now."

Aiden was surprised. He had known that the pastor didn't have much time to talk, but he was so eager for their conversation. Still he got up and followed the pastor back outside.

"You should come back Sunday and listen to my sermon. Perhaps you'll discover you still have some faith."

Aiden thanked him and said he would come back. It started to snow again. The wind created a tornado out of the flurries, but Aiden didn't mind. He knew he would have to get a new coat. His windbreaker just wasn't cutting it for this frigid weather. He figured he would worry about that concern later. He was feeling good about himself and he was worried about doing anything that would diminish the hope he had grown.

Aiden decided to go to the park. He did have mixed feelings about visiting that destination. He knew he would have flashbacks about the prosecutor, but maybe that was necessary. Aiden knew he would have to confront his guilt sometime. He had already accomplished so much today. Visiting his father and going to church. He got into his car and blasted on the heat. He rubbed his hands together. He pulled out of the church parking lot. As he drove he noticed the time and temperature was being given out on a giant electronic sign in front of a bank. There were still many hours in the day. Aiden couldn't believe it. He felt like he had been up for so long already. Aiden got to the park and pulled his car along the curb. There were more people outside. Enough time had passed for people to forget the violence. There was some atrocity being committed in every square inch of the metropolis not always a murder. It could have been a rape, an assault, or a mugging, but the civilians had grown numb. Sometimes they got mad.

Bartley would often encourage the police in his pocket to rough up civilians. His idea was that it would turn the public anger at the government and away from him. His plan had mixed success. The people were angry at the government, but any person with half a brain knew that it was Bartley pulling the strings. Even Aiden knew that when he was younger and idolized Bartley. The reason Aiden respected Bartley and why others respected Bartley were not for the reasons Bartley thought. Bartley thought people liked him because he was caring and gave money away to charity. It was true, he was a philanthropist, but that's not why Aiden originally liked him. Aiden liked Bartley because he saw someone crawl out of the muck. Bartley was born poor, but he became rich. He was the real deal. A true rags to riches story. It wasn't until he was older that Aiden realized Bartley only became wealthy because he stabbed people in the back.

Aiden got out of his car and started to walk towards the park. Aiden felt happy, but a little bit of fear was climbing its way up from his gut. He put one hesitant foot forward. *What are you scared of? Nothing terrible to you has happened. Get this over with.* Aiden swallowed the spit wallowing in his mouth and took a deep breath. He knew he could do this. A mother walked by with a baby. Aiden smiled at her. She grimaced back. Aiden forgot about his teeth. He always forgot about his teeth. Aiden continued. He thought. He hoped that maybe there would be less people in the woods. There weren't. That was stupid. Aiden should have known. People were everywhere. Why couldn't he just be alone? No. He didn't really think that. He was just afraid. He was always afraid. What the hell was wrong with him? He didn't know. His stomach was twisting in knots. The fear that had been climbing up from his gut now reached his throat. His mind was on fire. He started to panic.

He wanted to turn around and flee, but he stopped himself. *You can do this.* What was the problem? Aiden continued walking deeper into the forest. There was the familiar black cement path that snaked through the park. Most people were leaving. The sky was turning grey as mid-afternoon transitioned into night. The park was four square miles. Aiden thought he would walk the whole thing and clear his head. There was an avalanche of worrisome thoughts crushing his mind. He was coming to a point in his life where he didn't want to kill anybody anymore. He wasn't sure what else he could do. That was always the problem wasn't it? Aiden needed an out. He was looking for somebody to give him an option. Aiden stopped walking. He had come to the place where he had killed the prosecutor.

Aiden thought about the man's daughters. Aiden's eyes became wet. It felt so surreal. They weren't pouring down his face. He blinked a couple of times. It was hard to swallow. Aiden turned his head and looked at the bench near the spot where he murdered the prosecutor. He was a little surprised to see an old man wrapped in a thick wool coat and a fedora sitting there. To Aiden that spot was sacred. He walked up and sat down next to the man. The elderly person seemed harmless enough.

"You know somebody was killed here… right?"

The old man was short. Not much taller than five feet. He looked about eighty. He had a long droopy gizzard under his neck. The old man turned his head. He had a kind sparkle in his eyes. A small innocent smile. His smile wasn't directed at Aiden.

"I have come here to respect the dead."

"Is that so?"

"I visited the reporter last week."

"Why?"

"I try to visit the people in this city who have lost their lives to crime."

His face dropped. The kindness in his eyes was still there, but his smile was gone.

"My wife… she was shot in a drive by."

Aiden was quiet. Then he became confused. Mobsters didn't tend to kill civilians. It drew too much attention.

"What did she do?"

"She didn't do anything! She was a bystander."

There were always bystanders. The old man's cheeks had become wet. He wiped his face with his sleeve.

"Everybody was sorry. They gave me their sympathies. They didn't give me their time though. They didn't give me anything to make the pain go away. The police never even gave me her killers. All I have left is memories."

He sighed. He sounded like he might start crying again, but he collected himself. Aiden waited for the man to calm down. Aiden wasn't sure what to do. Except for his mother there never was anybody Aiden cared about.

"Now I try to visit all the murdered in this city. This city never provides me much time to do anything else. So many have died…"

"Has visiting these people actually helped anybody?"

"I'd like to think so. I counsel grieving families. I started up a support group. Many have suggested we lobby the government to do something. Our city is falling apart. There are activists for every cause. Philanthropists spend millions on starving children in third world countries. That's all fine and good, but they never think for a second about the problems going on all around them mostly because anybody with that much cash to burn hasn't been outside of their gated communities. I often wonder if these rich people aren't giving away money out of empathy, but so they can improve their own public image."

"I wouldn't say that's out of the question."

Aiden looked at the time on his phone. It was starting to get late.

"What do you think we should do? You think the regular people of this city should start fighting those trying to tear apart everything decent?"

Aiden sighed and stared deeply into the cold blue rolling water.

"I think that sounds dangerous. I've done so many terrible things in my life. I'm a criminal."

Aiden's eyes became wide. Had he said that? He thought he was only thinking it. He looked at Clarence. The old man didn't look stirred. He looked sympathetic.

"I've met people before who were criminals. Doing what I do now it's not so rare. They usually come to me purposefully. I didn't think I'd ever sit next to one by accident. I guess it is God's good graces."

Or statistical chance. Clarence reached into his coat. Aiden thought anybody who did this was about to pull out a weapon. If the person was old, young, male or female. Any sort of person could attack. Aiden didn't react. He wanted to. He was going to jump up and stop Clarence. The old man pulled out a card with a number written on it. He handed it to Aiden.

"What's this?"

"I got a friend. She's a reporter. She's been trying to investigate the crime in this city."

"This is your way of helping me?"

Clarence nodded, not catching the fact that Aiden was being sarcastic.

"Confession can be an enlightening experience. Plus it'll help this city. We need outside attention... I should probably get going."

Aiden nodded. He said goodbye, and watched
Clarence leave. Aiden put the card in his pocket. He
looked back at the river, entranced by the water. He pulled
out the bottle of pills Bartley had given him. He stared at it
for a while. He stood up and threw the bottle in the river.
Aiden watched the plastic bottle float away. Aiden stood
for a while. He leaned up against a tree. He wondered
what was happening to him. His phone rang. It was
Bartley.

"What do you want?"

"Can I meet you at your place?"

"Fine."

Aiden hung up. He got back to his station wagon, and
quickly got inside. He hoped his meeting with Bartley
would be short. He started to wonder why Bartley was
meeting with him. *Why didn't Bartley send over a
representative?* Aiden didn't let the thought bother him. He
turned on the radio. He listened to music to drown out his
thoughts. It was a much better alternative to shaking his
head. Aiden got back to the motel, and the girls were out.
Aiden didn't see Bartley's car. Bartley drove an expensive
sports car. Aiden supposed he could have driven
something more inconspicuous. Aiden got out and
brushed past the girls. Some of the newer women didn't
know who Aiden was. They would walk in front of him
and Aiden would push them out of the way so he could
get to his door.

Aiden got inside his room and fell on the bed. He
stared up at the ceiling for several minutes letting his mind
go blank. He didn't turn on the television. He didn't do
anything. He lay still not breathing not sure what he was
trying to accomplish. He wondered if there was anything
to meditation. Drifting away, and leaving your problems
behind you. At least that was Aiden's notion of

meditation. Aiden closed his eyes. He felt peaceful. He felt like he was going to fall asleep. He heard a knock on the door. He opened his eyes. The peace was gone. Aiden opened the door. Bartley stood in front of him. Aiden invited him inside. Bartley walked in and sat on the bed. He looked down at his feet. Aiden closed the door.

"What do you want?"

"I got one more job for you."

Aiden groaned.

"I mean the last one."

"What?"

Bartley looked up at him. Bartley smiled.

"That's what you wanted? That's as good an offer anybody in your profession gets. You know no such thing as retirement doing what you do."

"Why?"

"Good question."

Bartley pulled out a picture of a young girl not much older than sixteen.

"Who is she?"

Bartley looked away with a half-smile.

"I got myself into a real mess this time."

"Who is she?"

She was blond haired, blue eyed cheer leader type. Bartley shook his head back and forth.

"She was a stupid girl."

"Who is she?"

"She's pregnant."

"With whose child?"

Bartley turned his face back to Aiden. His half smile shrunk.

"Whose do you think?"

Aiden swallowed.

"I couldn't resist. She came on to me. She was pretty. She was there."

Aiden flipped the photo over. He saw an address on the back.

"She's staying with her parents at a cabin in Upstate New York. I'm not sure how she'll break the news. I can't let that happen. I've only thought of what would happen if they decided to find out who the father was. It would be alright if you limited it to just the girl, but if you have to get the parents too then so be it."

Aiden wasn't looking at Bartley. He had turned the photo over staring at the girl's face.

"Fifty grand."

"What?"

"Fifty grand. I've told Quinn. He's agreed to the job. He'll be here tomorrow night."

Bartley stood up and started for the door. Aiden was standing in front of him.

"Could you move?"

Aiden walked out of his way. Bartley thanked him.

"Listen. I'm prepared to give you fifty grand. It's not a lot, but I'm letting you go. Who gets an offer like that?"

Saturday, January 20th, 55 days left

Aiden awoke to a crack of sunshine that sneaked passed the shades and gently rested on his face. He stretched. His back cracked. He went to the bathroom scratching himself along the way. He looked at himself in the mirror. He started to wonder why he still had his beard. It was mangled and dirty. Several strands were knotted and clung together. Aiden needed to shave, but he didn't have a razor. He walked back to his bed. Under his pillow he kept a knife. Old precautions, but he couldn't sleep without it. Aiden cut the six inch strands that hung off his chin. He still had a beard, but now it wasn't so ghastly. Aiden figured he would do a better job after he had a razor, but first he had to think what he was going to do today. He called Deirdre. He sat on his bed and took out his phone.

"Hello?"

"What do you want?"

"I wanted to see you again."

He could hear Deirdre sigh.

"Listen Aiden," she began. She sounded like an adult conferring with a child. "I really don't know much about you. I think we should stop seeing each other. I mean you with your… job and my history with my father…"

"Okay. Okay. I know. I know. You're absolutely right, but listen to me. I'm done. It's over. I got one more job to do, and I'm retired."

"You'll never be retired. People like the man you work for will never let you go."

"It's different now. I know how the system works. Guys try to retire, and they're brought back in, but this time I get to leave. I'm the only person who's allowed to leave because my employer promised me. My reward is my release."

"You think you can trust this man?"

"I have a chance to escape and I'm not going to ruin it. I just want to see you again. That's all I ask. One date and then we can call it quits."

There was a long pause.

"Okay. We can go out this afternoon. If you're free?"

"I am."

"You can pick me up at four."

She told him her address and Aiden thanked her again. She hung up first. Aiden felt his heart fluttering. He took a shower and got dressed only to realize what he was wearing didn't qualify as dress clothes. Aiden would have to acquire something nicer. He started to clean his room. He wasn't sure where to start. He began by picking up a load of dirty laundry and shoving them into a black plastic trash bag. He could see the floor. He decided he would stop putting off his trip to the laundromat. He needed to continue cleaning. He started picking up garbage. There was mostly empty food packages. Chip bags, candy wrappers, and a couple of TV dinner boxes. Aiden discovered more than a few insects. There was a wet spot on the carpet along with a half-eaten chocolate bar. About a hundred ants had gathered near the vicinity. Aiden slew them all with a single stomp.

Aiden wiped his forehead which glistened with sweat. He was breathing heavily. What the hell had he done? Aiden never figured cleaning would wind up being such a disturbing and revealing activity. How had Aiden become such a slob? Aiden worked for the next few hours vacuuming and scrubbing the floor. He changed the sheets and left the door open so he could get rid of an ungodly smell he had unearthed when he started going through the mini-fridge. Sour milk and some mushy green glob that looked like it could have been at one point a vegetable. Everything had to go. There was no mercy. He threw everything out. He spared no snack or food. They were all tainted in Aiden's mind. The smell emanating from one of the plastic containers could knock a horse unconscious.

Aiden was almost done cleaning. That was the only thought that pushed him forward. He was almost done. *Think of Deirdre.* He had been cynical for so long. His life was finally turning around. His life was finally turning around. He kept repeating that statement in his head. It was the only thing keeping him sane. The thought that life could... that life would get better. His room was clean. He had yet to take the dirty clothes to the laundromat. He took a moment to catch his breath and decided it was time for him to leave. He picked up the trash bag full of his clothes and carried it out to the station wagon.

The laundromat was about ten minutes away. The vehicle puttered like usual before finally starting. Aiden checked the gas. He was on empty. Aiden drove to the first gas station he saw. It was full service. The man who came to his window was friendly looking. He tried to start a conversation.

"The weather's been nice. It hasn't snowed for a while. I live on a corner so I have to shovel twice as much sidewalk as anybody else. I'll tell you it's no fun."

"Yeah, I got a poor back. I don't have any sidewalk to shovel, but it sucks to drive in."

"I guess so. You know I don't drive that much. I don't live too far away."

"It must be awfully cold?"

"I bundle up thick with the help of my wife. You got a lady back home?"

"I hope so."

Aiden paid the man and got back on the road. He went to the laundromat. Put his clothes in the washer. He decided it would be awhile so he picked up a magazine and made himself comfortable on a nearby bench. There were several articles on the murders and violence in the city. It was national news. Even the federal government was promising a crackdown. Aiden doubted that crackdown would ever come. Politicians had promised for decades that crime would be eradicated. At best the authorities try to put a Band-Aid on a problem that required emergency care. They never got to the root of the issue. The washer started beeping and Aiden knew his clothes were done. He got up and put them into the dryer. He went back to the bench, picked up the article and continued reading.

The article went on to describe how outraged the government was at the ensuing turbulence in the region. There were five hundred murders a year. Only five hundred thousand people lived in the city. Aiden didn't know what the solution would be. He supposed crime and violence would always exist; unless you eliminated poverty, corruption, and cured mental illness. The dryer beeped. Aiden walked over and checked his clothes. They were warm. Aiden wished he could put them on. It was one of those simple pleasures Aiden couldn't get enough of especially when the weather got colder. He put the clean clothing back into the black trash bag and carried the bag out to his car. It was snowing again. Soon Aiden would be with Deirdre. He would get a nice suit and everything would be perfect. Aiden smiled. It disappeared almost as immediately as it had birthed. Aiden griped the stirring wheel tightly.

Thick heavy flakes descended gracefully to the ground. He could feel his heart being swallowed by darkness. Aiden wanted to go home. He wanted to crawl back in bed and sleep. Why? He was doing so well. Why was it now he started to feel anxious? It couldn't have been a coincidence. Aiden knew it wasn't. He felt like his life was going in the right direction. It felt like a dream. Aiden was worried that at any moment he might wake up.

Aiden went to a clothing store. He started looking at the fancier wear. He wondered what color he would look best in. Black or white? Those were the colors everyone picked. Aiden wanted to try something different. There was a light tan suit like Quinn had worn. He took it off the hanger. It was a little bit bulky on him. Aiden had a thin wiry frame. Nothing seemed to fit him very well. He had to wear belts all the time. Aiden tried on a different suit. This one fit better, but he didn't like the style. It was grey, made of wool, and had leather elbow pads. He just needed a pipe and a large academic book to complete the picture maybe sitting by a fireplace in an expensive looking red robe. He admired the picture he had created in his mind. He put the coat back on its hanger and looked for something else. A man came up to him wearing a uniform with the store's name and logo.

"May I help you sir?"

His comment made Aiden angry. Why did this man think he needed help? Did he look so clueless? *This man is trying to be nice.*

"I'm fine. Thank-you."

Human Beings are social creatures. We need to get a long just to survive. That is how we evolved. A much louder voice kept screaming *this is bad. Let him go. Let him go!* Aiden took a deep breath.

"Excuse me sir, but I may need help."

Aiden's pride contracted a little.

"I can't find any clothes my size. They're all too big. I'm not short. I need something that has long leggings and a small waist."

The man looked through a pile of several jeans.

"Would this one work?"

He handed Aiden a pair he had picked out of the bottom of the pile. Aiden nodded.

"I'll try those on, and I need a suit."

The man went back to the rack and searched through them all. He encountered one suit in the back and handed it to Aiden.

"This one might fit you."

Aiden thanked him. Aiden realized that if he had just looked a little bit longer then he probably would have found what he was looking for. *At least you forced yourself to talk to another human being, even if that person didn't have a choice but to talk back.* Aiden went to the changing room and tried on the clothes. They fit him well or at least as well as anything in the store would. He bought them and went back to the car. It was still snowing when he walked outside. It had piled up quickly.

How long had it been snowing? At least since he had left the laundromat. How long ago was that? Aiden looked at the time on his phone. It was nearly two. In fifteen minutes the snow was already passed his ankles. There had already been a considerable amount of snow on the ground when the flakes had started coming down. He continued his journey to the station wagon. He put the clothes in the back seat. He thought he would change when he got home. His car wasn't very good in this sort of weather. He needed to buy a new vehicle. He got back to the motel and he started to carry the clothes inside. He was so refreshed to open the door and not see a total mess. Why hadn't he done this years ago? He was mad at himself that he had procrastinated.

No use dwelling on things you don't have the power to change. I could have changed things though. I could have... He went to the bathroom and put on the new pants and suit he had bought. It still looked stiff on him. It would be a matter of time before the material conformed to his body. Aiden undressed and got back into his old clothes. He put the nice new ones on his bed where he hoped they wouldn't be ruined until after his date with Deirdre. There were only a few things he wanted to do. He drove the salon to get himself a haircut. He found it hard to breathe. Everything kept getting better. He told a woman standing near a cash register his name. She told him to have a seat and that it would be a few minutes before they were ready. A mother and her young son were sitting next to him.

"I'm getting a haircut today."

The woman gave a fake smile and nodded. She whispered something in the boy's ear. The boy got up and sat on the other side of her. Aiden didn't mind. He was feeling too good. Aiden picked up a book full of hairstyles. He flipped through the pages. They were all very beautiful. Even the guys had soft features and it was strange because the guys also tried to look tough. They wore leather jackets and smoked cigarettes, but rather than look like tough men they looked more like lesbians. There was no hair on their chests or faces. Aiden put the book down when he heard his name called. He followed a young girl to a seat in the back.

"Okay sir... what would you like?"

She swung a large sheet over Aiden's body.

"I'm really not sure what would look good. What do you think?"

The girl stared at his reflection for a minute or two.

"I think we could brush your hair back. Get it out of your eyes so we can see your face."

Aiden thought that plan was good enough. He thanked her and said he liked her idea.

"I would also like to shave my beard."

"All of it?"

"No mustaches, no goatees, and no muttonchops. I want it all gone."

Aiden relaxed as the girl did her job. He closed his eyes and sat back in his seat. The girl trimming his hair was not much older than the girl he would have to kill. His mind contracted. Aiden was already regretful. He didn't have all the details. Aiden would have to talk to Quinn, and he was pretty sure Quinn didn't have all the answers.

"How do you like it?" The girl asked taking off the apron.

Aiden looked at himself. The girl had brushed his hair to the back of his head. His hair had been greased. It was shiny and metallic looking. His clean shaven face still looked rough. His chin was like a jagged cliff edge. He looked less like a mangy dog and more like somebody had tried to groom a wolf.

"It's good."

It was an honest assessment. Aiden didn't think anybody could do much better with his looks. The girl who had been biting her lip nervously now looked relieved. Aiden got out of his seat and paid the bill. He gave the girl a large tip and left. He started to drive to Deirdre's house.

The Date

Aiden had never been to her house before, but he had several fantasies. He liked to imagine her living in a palace. It was a bad idea to romanticize the future. Reality was rarely as good as fiction. Sure enough when he got to her house there wasn't much to see. It didn't look terrible. It was on the eastside near the old industrial section. None of the houses in this part of the city were awful, but they were working class. Aiden parked next to the curb in front of her house. It was a tight fit. The cars behind and in front of him were a little too close together. It was hard not to touch them.

He looked at himself in the rearview mirror. He thought he looked acceptable. Deirdre was able to deal with him a few days ago when he still looked like his old sloppy self. He took a deep breath. He felt like he was stepping into frigid water. He felt cold all over. He hoped this nightmare would soon be over. He knocked on the door. He waited. And waited. He started to shift his stance. He scratched the back of his head. What was taking so long? He heard footsteps from inside. The door opened. Deirdre looked at him for a while. She wasn't smiling, but she opened the screen door and invited him inside. Deirdre's house was the opposite extreme of Aiden's motel room. It was a barren cold space. There was a single couch, a recliner, and a lamp in the room he was in and nothing else. There were no pictures on the wall, there was no television set, and not even a carpet. Just wooden floor boards.

"Are you renovating?"

"I don't like clutter."

Aiden started to feel a little frightened, but he tried not to show it.

"You may sit."

Aiden took a seat in the recliner. Deirdre sat down on the couch near him.

"So… is there anything you wanted to do?"

"I guess we could go out to eat."

"That's sounds good."

Deirdre got up and walked to a different section of the house. Aiden didn't get up, and he couldn't see where she went, but she came back shortly with a purse hanging off her arm.

"Are you ready to go?"

Aiden got to his feet. He walked slowly behind her as she stepped out the door.

"Who's car we taking?"

"We can go in mine."

Aiden followed Deirdre to her truck that was parked a couple spots behind his own vehicle. Aiden got into the passenger's side. Deirdre still looked serious, but she also seemed less tense. She turned on the radio, but kept the music low.

"So what have you been up to? You look good."

Aiden beamed. Everything he had done was paying off. He rubbed his arm.

"I've really been turning my life around recently. I feel like everything is coming full circle. I read an article once. It said most people are happiest in their lives by the age of thirty-seven. I'm almost fifty, and I never thought I could ever feel happy. Now things seem possible in my life that never seemed possible before."

She looked sympathetic. Any previous scorn she might have had evaporated. She put on a turn signal and transferred to a back road. Deirdre was the first person Aiden felt like he could lay all his problems on. He knew he shouldn't of, but she was patient with him. Deirdre didn't say anything back. Aiden was grateful. He didn't want his confession to be spoiled by a psychoanalysis. Deirdre stopped the car and put her hand on his shoulder.

"We're here."

Aiden looked out the window and realized they were in front of some bar on the Northside. It was a place he had never been to before. There were a lot of bars Aiden had never been to even though he had lived in the city his whole life. It didn't surprise him. There must have been the greatest concentration of drunks in his city than in any other area in a thousand miles. Also Aiden didn't drink.

Aiden and Deirdre stepped out of the car. They walked together. They were walking parallel until they reached the front door. Aiden stepped in front of her, and opened the door. She smiled at him and walked through. Aiden caught up with her. She reached out her hand and grabbed Aiden's. Aiden was surprised at first, but then he warmed up and started to clutch her hand too. Aiden looked down at her and she back up at him. Their moment was interrupted by a waiter.

"Excuse me, but would you two like a booth or table?"

"A table would be fine."

They were taken to a table in the back of the bar.

"What would you like to drink?"

"Water."

"You don't drink?"

Aiden shook his head. Deirdre ordered a wine. Her choice was cheap.

"You should order something better."

"I would, but the kind of wine I like really isn't that expensive."

Aiden didn't argue, but he wanted to. He wanted Deirdre to have the greatest. He imagined her in diamonds and fur coats, but then he realized that might diminish her specialness. Aiden wasn't attracted to glamorous women. He only wanted to spend money on Deirdre because he wanted her happy. Aiden didn't think there was anything he could do to make her more beautiful. The waiter left after they had made their decisions.

"So… why do you like cheap wine?"

Deirdre smiled and folded her hands together. She rested her chin on her fingers. She looked at Aiden with an intensive glare. Her eyes were wide. Aiden couldn't help but glow red. He wasn't sure why she was looking at him so intensely.

"You have gorgeous eyes."

"Excuse me?"

"Your eyes… I think they're really pretty."

Aiden was confused. He had heard a lot of people comment on his looks over the years. Pretty was an antonym for all of those descriptions. Aiden rubbed the back of his neck. He wasn't sure how to handle a compliment.

"Thanks?"

The words stumbled out of his mouth and fell flat on their face. Deirdre gave a small laugh and sat back in her seat.

"So tell me Aiden, what do you like to do?"

Aiden took a deep breath to prepare himself. He wanted to throw everything out at her. He wanted to just get the situation over with. Still he knew he had to calm down. He wished he could slap himself. He thought the action might seem odd and spontaneous to the people around him. His flesh was crawling. *Calm down.*

"I guess I like animals."

"Really?"

Aiden nodded. It was a stupid confession he thought, but it was honest. Aiden really did love animals. He hadn't owned a pet in decades because he didn't think he was responsible. He always wanted one. Aiden tried to elaborate.

"I've always liked animals. I had a pet bird once. It died after about a week."

"What happened?"

"A neighborhood kid snapped its neck."

Deirdre sat with her mouth open. A waiter came back.

"Is there anything on the menu that you liked?"

"I thought the chicken parmesan looked good."

The waiter looked over at Deirdre.

"What would you be having Mrs.?"

Both Aiden and the waiter gave her strange expressions like they couldn't understand what was wrong. She seemed upset. Aiden didn't know why. Was it because of the story? That happened decades ago. He didn't know why anybody except for him would care.

"Mrs.?" The waiter asked.

She got up and pushed the waiter out of her way.

"I can't... I can't do this."

The waiter still wasn't sure what was going on. Neither was Aiden. Deirdre kept walking till she left the bar. Aiden knew he had to catch her. He got up and started to run out the door.

"Sir... you have to pay, Sir!"

Aiden stopped and grumbled. He reached into his pocket and flung several dollar bills at the man. They floated down beside his feet. Aiden continued his pursuit of Deirdre. He saw she was almost to her car. Aiden continued running until he could grab her arm. As he touched her she turned around and slapped him. Aiden stepped back. He wasn't sure what he had done wrong.

"You can't do that!"

Aiden stood stupidly. The snow seemed to be falling around him. He never felt any of the flakes touch his skin. It was like he was wrapped inside a veil. He could see the world, but he couldn't touch it.

"I don't know what you mean."

Deirdre looked at him dumbfounded.

"How the hell...?" Her body stopped shaking. She relaxed, and brushed her hair back which had fallen in front of her face. She peered at Aiden with one eye. "Who are you?"

"What?"

"Why don't you act like you feel anything?"

"I haven't been around a lot of people. You were the first person who really seemed to care about me. I really want to make this relationship of ours work. I love you."

Deirdre had a stoic expression. Aiden wasn't sure what she would say. He wasn't sure what he had done wrong. Whatever it was he hoped she could forgive him. His heart was starting to beat fast, and he sweat despite a cold wind that was blowing on his face. Deirdre gave a half laugh that eventually transformed into a tired sigh. She rubbed her temple and put her head back.

"You love me... really? What do you even know about me?"

Aiden didn't know anything about her. Maybe speaking the truth hadn't been the right decision.

"I don't know anything about you. I just know you were kind to me. Really that's all. Yet that's enough."

Deirdre reached her hand around Aiden's neck and pulled him down so she could kiss his forehead.

"Come on, I'll take you home."

They didn't talk much in the car. Deirdre had turned on the radio. Some soft classical music was playing. Aiden wanted to ask Deirdre if he could see her again, but he thought the time wasn't right so he looked out the window and watched the scenery pass. They were coming from the north, so the buildings and people began to look sketchier. Everything deteriorated. Aiden was back at his car. He looked at Deirdre as she pulled onto her street.

"Will I see you again?"

Deirdre looked uncertain. Aiden felt like there were invisible fingers clenching his throat.

"I need to be honest with you. I'm leading you on. I don't want to be a tease. I really do like you, but considering my past I'm not so sure being in a relationship with you is a good thing. I don't even think knowing you is a good thing."

Aiden felt like there was a wall crumbling inside of him. He thought he would turn to dust. Like his soul had been cracked. He put his head down.

"I know what it's like you know. To be betrayed. If you're anything like me I'm guessing you don't have anybody in your life. I'm guessing if you're like me than being in a relationship might be frightening, but I'm guessing if you're like me than being alone is frightening. I'm teetering on a tightrope, and no matter which way I lean I'm afraid I'm going to fall."

"I can come back… If you want me too. I just need you to promise me you'll stop. You're not going work for the mob doing whatever it is that you do. I don't even care if you serve drinks at a mob bar. You have to quit… I think it would break me if somebody else betrayed me again… This is going to sound insane… But I'll be here when you've quit."

Aiden smiled at her, but he said nothing. He got out of the truck. Aiden got back into his station wagon and drove to the motel. He sat down on his bed. Once again he was glad he had cleaned. Why hadn't he done it sooner? It was an old question he kept asking himself. There wasn't a point anymore. He pulled his phone from his pocket. He decided to call Quinn. He was ready to get the job over with.

"Hello?"

"Yes… It's me. I want to deal with this girl now."

Quinn told him he would be right over. Aiden waited. He didn't turn on any lights. He figured Quinn would be there soon enough so he sat in the darkness and contemplated the situation. He heard a car door shut outside. Aiden got up and went over to discover the black van was waiting for him. Aiden sighed and walked out. He saw Quinn in the driver's seat. Aiden got into the passenger's seat. Without a word Quinn started to drive away. Aiden rested his head in his hand and looked out the window. It was quiet inside the vehicle. Aiden didn't want to talk anyway, but it was Quinn who attempted to initiate a conversation.

"So... are you going to be okay? Do you have any work you can do after this?"

"Shut up and drive."

Aiden started to think about the girl. He wondered if he would be able to do it...

"I've never killed anybody so young."

"I haven't killed anybody. Ever!"

Aiden thought about reassuring him, but thought reassurance would be wrong. What they were doing was wrong. Quinn should feel guilty.

"Quinn? When I'm gone can you promise me to leave Bartley as soon as you can?"

"I've made my choices... Someday I'll pay for those choices."

It was the one thing Aiden didn't want to hear. The same thing Aiden felt at Quinn's age.

"Things can change. People can change. You can make your life better."

"Shut up, I'm driving."

Aiden sighed and slid deep into his seat. He knew the trip was going to be another four hours. He didn't attempt to stay awake. He dreamt of Deirdre. He dreamt he was living with her. He dreamt he was in her bed.

"We're here."

Aiden rubbed his eyes. He sat up. He had been hunkered low and had wrapped himself around his seat belt. Aiden looked out his window. There was snow all around them. Aiden couldn't even see the road, but instead an endless sheet of white that extended all around them for miles.

"Where are we?"

"We are off route… luckily I have all wheel drive and already chained my tires while you were in dreamland. We're staying in a hut. I brought camping supplies. The girl and her family's cabin aren't too far away."

Aiden couldn't believe it. Had time flown so fast?

"Why isn't this girl in police protection?"

"She's obviously more concerned about the retaliation of her parents. To be fair it's a little hard to be intimidated by that fat imp."

"Won't her parents know she's pregnant?"

"Maybe she intended to get an abortion before she got too big."

They reached the outskirts of a forest on the end of the massive white plain.

"The girl's cabin is on the other side of these woods."

Aiden got out of the car and Quinn did too. Aiden looked around. They were in the middle of nowhere. It didn't seem like there was civilization for a million miles. Aiden looked behind him. In the far distance was the outline of a mountain shrouded by a thick evening mist. Aiden continued to follow Quinn into the woods. The shed which Quinn had picked out didn't even look like it could fit two people standing. Quinn pulled out a long box with a picture of a tent on the front. There were two sleeping bags. Aiden walked into his hut and saw a cot which swallowed the majority of space. There was a small heater in the corner that took what little room was left.

"Were you expecting the Hilton? It's your last job. Be thankful that everything will be over soon."

Aiden grumbled, but he didn't complain. He went right onto the cot after unrolling his sleeping bag. There weren't blankets, pillows, or even a sheet on the cot. Aiden knew this would be a stripped down existence. He hated the outdoors. After Quinn had set up his tent he came back to check on Aiden. He poked his head through the door.

"The killing begins tomorrow."

Sunday, January 21st, 54 days left

Aiden didn't want to think. He turned on the heater and tried to fall asleep as quickly as he could. The winds raged outside. A tsunami of white bashed against a small window above his head. Aiden closed his eyes and drifted off. He had no dreams. He wasn't asleep long enough. He heard a banging on the door. It was morning. Aiden thought they were attacking at nighttime. They always attacked at night. It's the daytime?

"Why the Hell are we attacking in the daytime?!"

"It's three in the morning! It looks like the daytime because of the snow."

Aiden grumbled some more, but he got up. He walked over to the door. He was already dressed. He hadn't changed or showered in a couple of days. You didn't have to look fancy for a murder.

"How far away is the cabin?"

"We have about an eight mile walk ahead of us."

"Do we have to kill the parents too?"

"I can't see a way around it. There all spending time together. An opportunity like this doesn't come often. Our targets are all together and isolated."

Aiden sighed. Quinn was already fully dressed in expensive looking hiking gear. All Aiden had was a simple track suit and jeans. Quinn was holding a walking stick. A handgun was attached to his hip.

"I was not prepared for this."

"I packed you some appropriate wear in the van. I'll give you ten minutes to change. We don't have much time.

This isn't like back home where we have the police watching our backs. We have to be careful. We don't know if the family is going to leave or not today. They shouldn't. Today there is a huge blizzard."

Aiden couldn't deny it. He was impressed.

"Have you been to the range?"

"I can hit the bull's-eye nine times out of ten."

"That's no indication of how good you are. Wait until your blood starts flowing, and you don't even realize what you are doing. The worst moment comes afterward when you don't have that adrenaline. When you come to your senses and realize you just killed a person. People usually don't die right away. They linger to life. That's the moment when you have to walk over and finish them while they are begging for mercy. We're killing a child... I'm sure the parents will do everything in their power to persuade you to resist. You can't."

"I know that!"

"Nobody is ever ready for these sorts of things. Even somebody who feels no guilt when they kill is surprised by the outcome. Death really isn't ever how you expect it. I've killed a dozen people up close, and it's all different. Some die quickly and some die slowly, but none of them die with dignity."

Quinn was starting to look worried. He looked like he wasn't sure of himself.

"You're finally showing the right emotion."

"What's that?"

"Fear."

Aiden put his hand on Quinn's shoulder who was now looking incredibly down.

"Why don't you take me to the van so I can get the equipment?"

Quinn nodded, and started to walk away. Aiden followed him. There was a large sack he slipped over his arms. Aiden hadn't ever been backpacking before. He didn't know what it was like, but he knew that snow was the most difficult terrain. Aiden picked up a shotgun and three grenades. He shut the back doors after asking Quinn if there was anything else he needed.

"Are you ready to go?"

Quinn nodded, but his movement was subtle and withdrawn. Aiden slung the shotgun over his back. They started hiking. For the first hour Aiden said nothing. His legs began to hurt and he felt out of breath. Quinn and Aiden came to a hill. Aiden realized the trip to the girl's cabin was going to be more difficult than he realized.

"Are we almost there?"

Quinn had recovered from his withdrawn attitude. He smiled and looked behind him to see Aiden desperately trying to catch up.

"You've never explored the great outdoors before?"

Aiden quickly took a few large steps forward till he was next to Quinn, and kept walking till he was ahead.

"You're a hell of a lot younger. In my prime I would have kicked your ass."

"Is that so? We're about a half mile away… you think you can make it?"

"You're the one behind me!"

They were at the top of the hill. Aiden could see the cabin. A small brown dot in the distance surrounded by a sea of white. There was a thin silver curvy road that extended beyond the cabin. He looked at Quinn.

"This'll be your last job with me. After this your own your own."

Quinn nodded. His face was blank. Aiden couldn't tell if he was scared or not. If he was then he was doing a good job of hiding it.

"I attack from the front. You attack from the back. I'll shout when I attack."

"What will you shout?"

"It doesn't matter. When you hear me screaming then you go in guns blazing, but we can't talk until that moment comes."

Aiden continued in the direction of the cabin. He worried somebody might see him. There didn't appear to be too many windows. Aiden was wearing white clothing so he blended in nicely with his environment. The closer he got to the cabin the lower he got. When he was within fifty feet of the cabin he started to crawl. He looked back to see Quinn. The boy followed Aiden's actions. He told Quinn to go in the opposite direction. He mouthed his instructions. Quinn nodded and began to crawl away. There was one window Aiden saw, and he knew he would have to hug the ground the rest of his journey.

After a few more minutes agonizingly forwarding on his elbows, Aiden was just beneath the window he had seen in the distance. Aiden lifted up just a little bit so he could sit on his knees. He heard the bones in his legs crack. *Jesus!* Aiden gave a small peak inside the window. He knew he would have to be quick. His heart was racing. Was this a good idea? It was certainly risky. Aiden held his breath and popped his head up. He looked through the glass for only a second before driving his face back into the snow. It was enough time to check what was going on.

He saw a bedroom with a girl lying on her stomach on her bed. She had headphones on and was listening to music on a CD player. She was also looking over a notebook. Perhaps she was doing schoolwork? Aiden couldn't see a bump on her belly. Why had she been so careless? Was she looking for adventure? Probably. This girl got herself into trouble. She deserves what happens. *She is still a child.* Aiden shook his head free of the thought. He had a job to do. It was his last job and then he could be done. There was no way out of this situation. *You could turn yourself in.* Aiden shook his head. Of course he couldn't do that. It was ridiculous. With the things he's done he would get the death penalty. *Not if you confess.*

"I'm not going to prison!"

He quickly covered his mouth with his hand. He hadn't meant to talk aloud. He had to be quiet. He managed to focus himself. He started crawling to the end of the cabin. He peered around. He saw a black truck in the driveway. Aiden had learned a lot about cars over his career. It was one of the better ways to kill people. To cut their breaks or wire their engine with a bomb. Both kinds of killings he didn't have to get close. This wouldn't be one of those times.

He pressed his ear against the wooden wall. He could hear footsteps from inside. The greatest danger now was if somebody for any reason decided to step outside. He wasn't sure why anybody would. It was a freezing unfriendly day. The sort of day Aiden wished he could stay inside for. But it would just be his luck if he was discovered. He wasn't sure if these people had guns. They seemed like a redneck family. Aiden wasn't sure when the right time was to attack. He tried to control his breathing. He kept lurching forward, but then stopping himself. Aiden heard a door open. He scurried around the other side of the truck. He prayed he wouldn't be seen. It seemed odd to him that God would protect him so he could later murder these people. Aiden supposed it was an instinctual reaction. He peaked under the truck and he could see a man's feet on the steps of the cabin's porch. He heard a woman's voice call from inside.

"Randy? What are you doing?"

"I'm getting a book from the car."

"Come here and be social."

Aiden could hear the man sigh and turn around, but before he did he took a pack of cigarettes and buried it in the snow. He had his back to Aiden. If he turned around then Aiden would be discovered. Aiden's heart beat against his chest so hard he thought it was trying to escape his rib cage. The man stood up and went back inside. He didn't shut the door completely. Aiden released the air that had been building up in his lungs. He started running. Several thoughts rushed through his head. *Don't do this, don't do this!* One thought chimed. *Do this and you can be with Deirdre,* another thought retorted. Aiden chucked a grenade before he entered. He dived into the snow bank and started counting silently to himself…3…2…1…

The family had been sitting close together. The father was on the couch reading a newspaper. The mother was in the kitchen checking the oven. The girl was just entering the living room. They had turned their heads slightly only to receive a brief glimpse of a stranger chucking something into their house. Aiden covered his ears. There was an enormous blast. Not much fire in the explosion. Just a grey cloud mixed with wood dust and snow. He picked up his shotgun and charged inside.

"Now!"

Quinn broke through the back door, and Aiden went through the front. When the father moaned he quickly swiveled on his feet and pulled the trigger. There was a loud boom. Aiden could feel the sound in his stomach. The pellets ripped through the man's face. Quinn flinched even though he hadn't been the one who fired. The mother was already dead. A pool of blood collected on the floor and out from a hole in her stomach. Quinn looked up at Aiden. He looked like he might get sick. He hadn't even killed anything.

"Was that it?"

The daughter moaned. She was lying on her stomach and clutching her leg. A fragment from the grenade had pierced her calf. Quinn's face became as white as the corpse's lying around them.

"Shoot her!"

Quinn was shaking uncontrollably, but he stepped forward and put his boot on her neck; her face was smashed against the floor. She was crying and wailing. The winds assailed them. Quinn's hair blew in front of his eyes. The storm had come. Aiden looked out the open doorway he had just bashed through. The wind was blowing so fast that it created a shrill whistling noise and the snow flooded the inside of the cabin. A quarter of a foot had already piled up in the few seconds Aiden spent staring. Aiden returned his attention to the girl and Quinn. The revolver shook in his hands. The muzzle was going in circles and then in a zigzag direction…

"Just pull the trigger!"

"I've got a baby!"

The girl went back to crying. Aiden heard the bang of Quinn's gun. The crying stopped. Quinn opened one eye to inspect the carnage he had created. There was a massive indentation in the girl's head. Quinn collapsed on his knees. His hands fell limply by his side. The revolver landed with a thud on the ground.

"...I..."

The single word peaked and fell like a wave. The blizzard looked fierce. It would be a while before anybody would reach the cabin, but the police would come sooner or later. Aiden decided to wait a few minutes and see if Quinn could collect himself. Quinn... the boy. His exposure fell apart like an old wall. Aiden walked over to him and put his hand on the boy's shoulder.

"It gets worse the second time..."

Quinn wiped the snot and tears off his face with the back of his sleeve. Aiden was already walking out the door. Aiden thought Quinn would be soon to follow, but he didn't. Aiden turned around. Quinn was still kneeling. He leaned over and his face was near the girl's. Her head was cradled in his hands. Blood from her temple streamed between his fingers.

"I'm sorry."

Quinn put her head back down on the ground.

"I'm ready to go."

It was a lonely walk back. The wail of the wind started to sound like human screams. The snow was blinding. Aiden kept following the vague outline of Quinn's body.

"Are we almost to the hill?"

Quinn shouted something back, but Aiden could not hear. He did start to feel an inclination beneath his feet. They had reached the hill. Aiden squinted. He could see an evergreen tree not far away. Quinn was sitting on the ground.

"I can't move."

Aiden stood there looking down at him.

"I can't move."

Aiden knew what he meant. Aiden had felt the same thing. It had been decades, but the impression was hard to remove. Aiden sat down in front of Quinn. He leaned back against a tree. It felt good to sit.

"I have to stop. I have to go back."

"You can't."

"What should I do?"

"Keep going. Right now is not the time to grow a conscience. The girl made bad choices."

They sat in silence for a while.

"Her name was Jessie."

"What?"

Her name was Jessie. Bartley told me her name when he was describing the job

"Okay, okay…"

Quinn eventually nodded and tried to stand up. His legs wobbled. Aiden grabbed his hand.

"How do you do it?"

"Do what?"

"You know."

Aiden did know.

"I don't ever think about it."

They kept walking. They talked no more. They reached the hut and Quinn's black van. It seemed so much shorter than the first trip. Aiden's mind was a blank slate. He tried not to think about anything. Every action seemed preprogrammed. Quinn imitated Aiden's behavior. The events of the morning seemed like a forgotten dream. In Aiden's hazy state he wasn't sure if anything had actually happened. Could it?

"You okay driving?"

"Yeah I'm... fine."

Aiden got into the passenger's seat. He didn't fall asleep. Aiden felt like he was already asleep. He watched the road. The dashed endless line that divided the highway. It was transfixing. It almost looked like a stone that skipped in a pond. Aiden hadn't felt this way in decades. Quinn parked the car. Aiden looked over at Quinn and saw him getting out of the van.

"We need gas."

Aiden got out of the van too. It felt good to stretch his legs. It was late at night. Aiden couldn't believe how quickly time had passed. He didn't fall asleep or at least he didn't think so. Aiden was hungry. He looked at the gas station and saw a collection of snack stands. He eagerly sought out a bag of chips.

As he was about to walk inside, a large woman in a tank top barged her way past Aiden. She was huge. At least three hundred pounds. She looked like a piece of gum that had been chewed for hours. All the flesh was hanging off her figure like thick slime. She was drinking a liter of soda. She was pouring it straight into her mouth. She didn't even look like she cared if anybody saw her. Aiden realized they must be close to home. He looked at the time on his phone. It was nearing one in the morning. How had time become so diluted? It seemed like it was morning not that long ago. Aiden wasn't hungry anymore. He felt confused and panicky. Quinn came back out. He was putting his wallet back into his pants pocket.

"You want me to drive?"

Quinn shrugged and handed over the keys. After about an hour Aiden could see a sign welcoming them to their home city. Aiden scoffed. What kind of greeting they had. It was a lie. Their city had no wonderful landmarks despite its three hundred year old age. There were a couple stone buildings from the revolutionary period, and the silhouettes of the skyscrapers in the North stood proudly above the meager buildings in the south. The factories that weren't shut down during the recession produced so much smoke that it seemed like somebody had just burned the place down. It looked like it was a medieval village that had just been plundered.

"How often have you been outside the city?"

"Never."

"Why did you decide to work for Bartley?"

"Bartley was willing to pay me a good sum, better than a garbage man, my alternative career. It was exciting. I glorified Bartley. He did for me what my parents never could. Then I started to see things." Quinn lowered his head in shame. "I've seen people die. I've seen people die badly, but it's all been put into perspective today. I'm the one who did it. I killed Jessie."

Monday, January 22nd, 53 days left

They were almost to Bartley's tavern. Aiden parked the van about a block away.

"I'm going to walk home."

Aiden extended his hand and Quinn shook it. They both got out of the van. Aiden kept walking to the tavern. It was the first time he had ever looked at it with joy. Even when he was younger, and he had all these misconceptions about gang life. He had never stared with such anticipation. He walked around back to the entrance, cut through the long line, and ignored the contemptible glares of others who had been waiting to get in long before him. Mike the guard let him through. He looked at Aiden strangely. He saw Bartley. He was sitting at the same table he was always at. A band playing jazz was behind him. However Bartley didn't look happy like he usually did. He started staring bitterly at Aiden with his hands folded and resting on the table.

"It's over?"

Aiden nodded. Aiden kept waiting. Was Bartley going to pay him? After all that sin he had committed for the imp? Aiden clenched his fist. He remained calm. He never forgot how powerful Bartley was.

"Are you going to pay me?"

"I don't know."

"You promised."

"What is your point?"

"You ever hear of the Praetorian Guard? They guarded the Roman Emperor."

"Is that so?"

"They weren't very good at their job."

"Why's that?"

"The Praetorian Guards killed when they were mistreated."

Bartley gave a half smile and looked one of the armed men. Aiden was handed a hefty envelope. He didn't need to look inside. Aiden stood up, and began walking away. Aiden saw Quinn enter just as he was about to leave. Aiden folded the envelope and put it in his pocket. He nodded to Quinn. Quinn smiled back. Aiden was across the street walking home when he heard a voice call his name. Aiden turned around. It was Bartley. The imp waddled over. He ran quickly before a car came. He looked vulnerable. His head was down. The wind bashed against him like a wave. He stared down at his feet.

"What do you want?"

Bartley looked up. He had tears in his eyes. Aiden was shocked. This tough little man had broken down. He smiled. He looked left of him at the rising sun.

"She was a good girl..."

"Her name was Jessie."

"What?"

"Her name was Jessie."

"I know that. I've ruined so many lives. So many young boys don't have a future because of me. So many young boys aren't alive because of me. I'm going to end it one of these days. You ever think about doing it?"

Aiden didn't answer. He stared in the opposite direction of the sunlight.

"Are you done?"

"Yeah, I'm done."

There was a suburban community Aiden knew of. It was a nice set of identical row homes. It had been decades since he'd been there. It wasn't far away from where he was walking. He knew a girl from the area. He had dated her for a while. He wasn't sure why she was interested in a boy from his area. She lived in a much nicer place then he did. Aiden was thuggish. She never introduced him to her parents. She said they were uptight.

Aiden thought of the girl in the cabin. There was something about rich girls and danger Aiden couldn't understand. The girl he knew stopped seeing him after her parents found out about the relationship. Aiden didn't think her parents were prejudice against slum folk, but they had their misconceptions. They were the sort of people who would donate plenty to charity, but lock their doors when a suspicious person walked by their car. Aiden didn't even know Bartley at that time. He was fifteen, but he figured if people were going to treat him like a criminal than he might as well be one. Now Aiden thought differently. He wondered if things had changed. He met Deirdre. She was a girl in the north who wasn't afraid of him. Maybe life could get better. Aiden visited the suburbs where he had met that rich girl he dated. Would the neighborhood be as alien as it once seemed?

This was the dream wasn't it? Struggle and bleed. Rise past the status of your birth. Aiden looked at one of the houses. It was gigantic. Not necessarily tall, although it was that. Beyond three stories, but it was wide and long. There were huge bay windows. Only the rich had those kinds of windows. The kind that graciously allowed outsiders to view the inside of their home. Aiden kept walking. So many nice homes. A man outside dressed in a thick bathrobe was getting the newspaper. He was fat and balding.

"You lost, sir?"

The man didn't ask in a friendly manner. Aiden remembered why he had stayed away from the place for so long. No, sir. He started walking away. Aiden's walk was interrupted by a strong wind. It was snowing again. *Fucking Snow.* He sighed. Why was he so pissed? Why was he so nervous? He took out his phone. He wondered if he should call Deirdre. *Go on.* Aiden dialed her number. He waited impatiently for it to ring. Come on, he muttered tapping his foot. Aiden leaned against a telephone pole.

"Hello?"

"Hi, I'd like to see you again."

"Come over to my house. I need to show you something."

Aiden was curious. He didn't ask. He didn't like surprises, but if Deirdre wanted to reveal the mystery in person then Aiden wouldn't stop her.

"Okay then; I'll see you later?"

"Yeah."

She hung up. Aiden started walking a little faster with his chin a little higher. He was almost to Deirdre's. Aiden began to relax. *What does she want to tell me?* He was at her house. Aiden took a wobbly step forward. He didn't want to know what was inside. It could be good. *What in your experience would ever suggest that?* Aiden knocked.

"Come in."

Aiden turned the knob. He was afraid to push the door open. What would he see? *Stop procrastinating.* He took a deep breath and opened the door. Deirdre was sitting on the couch. She had a toddler in her arms. It was wearing light blue suspenders. It was drinking...*stop* *calling him it...*The *boy* was sitting on her lap drinking a bottle of apple juice.

"Is that yours?"

"His name is Ben. I'm sorry I didn't tell you sooner. I guess we all have are secrets. I was a hypocrite."

Aiden sat down next to her. He carefully put his arm around her shoulders.

"Your secret was completely understandable. I'm a crook you really don't know, and that's your child."

Aiden wasn't sure if it was right of him to ask who the father was.

"Do you like kids?"

"I've never really known any kids."

"You were a kid though, right?"

Aiden wasn't sure how to answer that question either, but he said yes. Ben smacked his lips. Deirdre started to hand Ben over to Aiden.

"What are you doing?"

"I want you to hold him."

"I'm not sure that's a good idea, I've never held a kid before. What if I hurt him?"

Deirdre gave a small snicker and continued to hand the baby over. Aiden took the baby, but was still arguing.

"You're not going to hurt him."

"Yes, but..."

Ben was already in his arms. Aiden was going to complain again, but he thought it was useless. He looked down. He became immediately protective of the small creature. He felt like he was holding an expensive vase.

"He's cute."

Deirdre got up.

"I'm thinking of furnishing this place up. I'd like it to be less empty."

"Yeah... that sounds like a good idea." Aiden was not really paying attention. He was afraid Ben would start crying if he wasn't being rocked. Deirdre walked out of the room and Aiden grew nervous.

"Hey wait, where are you going?"

She didn't answer. She came back out with a picture and sat next to Aiden. She showed him the photograph. Aiden saw Deirdre, Ben, and a man Aiden didn't recognize in his early thirties wearing a wife beater.

"That's Ben's father?"

"He... was a crook."

"I know how to choose them don't I?"

Aiden looked at her, struggling to say something comforting, but getting his tongue tied up instead.

"What did he do? You don't have to say anything if you don't want to."

"No... I want to get this over with. He was a street thug. He beat people. I always knew he did. I never questioned him. He wasn't awful to live with. There wasn't anything about him to enjoy either. Ben was born and he split. I haven't seen him since." Deirdre brushed away a strand of hair behind her ear. "I just want a normal life. I've made so many strides. My son is all I have left in the world. I'm like one of those deranged mothers that hang onto their children because they feel like getting knocked up is an achievement. I'm not even going to blame my father. I'm tired of blaming people for my problems."

"I think you're way ahead of me. I blame people all the time. I can't accept the things I've done in my life. Everything is a mess. You couldn't choose your father. You weren't responsible for the things your child's father did. You haven't harmed anybody. It seems to me that plenty of people have harmed you."

"You're a good person, aren't you?"

"A person like you should never condemn yourself. You don't know the things I've done."

"You were desperate. Now you've quit. I thought my life was going to hell again. I couldn't let that happen with a son at home."

Aiden suddenly needed to tell her the truth.

"I killed a young girl. Her name was Jessie."

The words did not come out. He tried to open his mouth, but still nothing happened. *Tell her.* Aiden didn't. Deirdre looked at him seeing a man who was trying to get his life together. That was one truth. The other truth was a man who had done horrible things. Things no man should ever be forgiven for.

"I want you to live with me."

"I can't."

"Why not?"

"I'm going to hurt you."

"I've been hurt enough, Aiden. You are the only thing I hope can stop me from hurting anymore."

"I have to think about this."

Aiden stood up and went outside. He didn't look back. He felt like he was being smothered. He needed to feel the cold air on his face. He stood on Deirdre's front porch. He was panicking. He felt sick. Was he going to throw up? *You need to tell her the truth.* I can't. *You need to.* Aiden was breathing faster. I'm done. I'm never going to hurt anybody ever again. Why can't I be happy? Why can't I leave my past alone? I'm done. Give me peace! *You can't have peace.* He went back inside and knelt by Deirdre's side. He held her hand and looked into her eyes.

"I want to live with you, but only if that will make you happy."

"I would be overjoyed."

"I would be too, but for how long? Every time I've experienced happiness it escapes."

Deirdre touched his face. *She doesn't know about the things you've done. Leave her alone.* Aiden jumped up. His legs were wobbly. He stumbled over to the door. He put his fingers loosely around the handle. He looked back at Deirdre. He didn't want to leave her.

"I have to collect my things. I won't be long."

"I'll be here when you get back."

<u>Abandoned</u>

Aiden got to his car. He thought he was floating on air. Everything felt so surreal. He didn't even feel the cold. He drove in silence. He kept thinking about the future. A concept he usually tried to push out of his mind. He looked forward to tomorrow. Aiden was still trembling like he was afraid. He stared at the rippling skin of his arms. Why was this happening to him? This was the one moment in his life when he shouldn't be scared. Aiden approached the motel. His heart beat faster no matter how much he tried to rationalize the situation. The girls were out again crawling out of whatever dark crevice spawned them.

Aiden parked in front of his room. He started going inside. All that cleaning Aiden supposed was for nothing. Now he wouldn't be living here. Aiden walked in and decided to only take the necessities. What did he hold most dear? Aiden realized he owned nothing of value. He packed his clothes. He put away his guns in the trunk. He knew he would have to dispose of those later. He picked up anything else he thought he might need. Toothbrush, toothpaste, Washcloth. Family pictures. Just his mother. After all his moving he wondered if maybe he should just burn everything. He knew the idea was crazy, but he wanted to leave everything behind him. Every item that might remind him of his old life. What did he need anyway? He didn't have any memorabilia except for his mother. Aiden put everything in the station wagon.

He was about to drive to Deirdre's, but he saw a girl sitting on the curb, crying. She looked like one of the younger ones. Aiden had lived at the motel for so many years. He had never paid much attention to the girls. Now though, now that he was leaving? Watching the girl made his heart bleed. He sighed and walked over. He sat down next to her. She had a tissue in her hands. She was sobbing nonstop. Aiden wasn't sure what to say. The girl didn't even seem to notice him. She wasn't dressed like the older women. She didn't wear much make-up. She wore short-shorts, skate shoes, and a tank-top. Her long red hair was brushed to the left of her head and flowed down on her shoulder like a waterfall. Aiden coughed.

"What's wrong?"

The girl stopped crying for a moment. She looked over. She stared at Aiden for a minute, and then she looked in the other direction. Was he talking to her? The girl wiped her eyes with the back of her arm.

"I... I didn't get paid. I didn't please one of the customers. So... Jimmy didn't give me my... my..."

She started sniffling. She started crying again. Aiden sat awkwardly. He didn't know what to do. The girl put her arms around him. Aiden was surprised, but then eventually put his arms around her.

"It's okay."

"How do you know?"

Aiden sighed and looked back at the motel.

"I guess I never thought things would ever be okay. I still don't, but there's no point in giving up. You got to get your life together."

The girl shook her head. She looked terrified.

"I can't… I can't."

She swallowed. Aiden raised an eyebrow.

"How old are you?"

"Sixteen."

"Damn…"

The girl looked unsure if she should explain.

"I'm not going to rat you out."

The girl still looked skeptical.

"I ran away."

"Why?"

"My mother used to…she used to…"

The girl started crying again. Aiden grumbled.

"Stop it. Stop it!"

The girl stopped. Aiden sighed.

"Did this really seem like the better option?"

The girl shook her head.

"What else can I do?"

"I don't know."

The girl squinted her eyes. She pointed a finger.

"I know you. You're the one who never buys. Why are you talking to me now?"

"…Because I'm leaving."

"Why didn't you care before?"

"…Because you were just the scenery."

Aiden stood up. He looked down at the girl. She had finally collected herself. Aiden gave her a hand so she could get to her feet.

"What's your name?"

"Jamie."

"It sounds like Jessie."

"I guess it does."

The girl laughed, but Aiden didn't. He looked at his station wagon. He reached into his pocket and pulled out his wallet.

"How much do you usually get?"

"Sixty. Where do you want to go?"

"I'm going home."

"You don't want any service?"

Aiden shook his head. He noticed the girl's skin was blue. He took out a hundred dollar bill.

"Buy yourself a coat."

Aiden turned around and went to the station wagon. He sat in his seat without putting the key in the ignition. He watched Jamie. She walked over to an older boy who was leaning against a lamp post. She handed him several dollar bills. The older boy gave her a zip-lock baggy. Aiden couldn't see what it was specifically, but he didn't need to be up close.

"Stupid girl..."

Deirdre's house wasn't far. He could envision it already. That's where he would be living. In her bed? Aiden's heart beat faster. He couldn't go yet. He couldn't. He made a sharp left turn. The car behind him honked. He was going to the park. Aiden was on an empty back road, but he was driving ninety. The speed limit was thirty. He slammed his foot on the breaks. What was he doing? He continued driving although at a slower, steadier pace. Aiden parked his station wagon in a nearby lot. There weren't many people around. A skinny old cat with a missing eye darted in front of him as Aiden opened his door. Aiden let out a surprised gasp.

"Where the hell did you come from?"

The black cat started pacing back and forth around Aiden's leg.

"Go on. Get out of here."

The feline was persistent. Aiden continued forward. He ran into the woods. He heard a meow. He saw the cat following him. Aiden ignored the creature and continued jogging down the black cement path that weaved throughout the woods. Aiden got to the bench where he had killed the prosecutor. Where he had met Clarence.

Aiden sat down. He was looking at the river. Still frigid looking. Aiden wondered if the prosecutor's ghost would come take its vendetta. Aiden didn't believe in ghosts let alone vengeful spirits and Aiden thought he was pretty low on the list of mass murderers. Hitler. Pol Pot. Osama bin laden. None of these people ever disappeared mysteriously in the middle of the night. Osama Bin Laden did, but that wasn't from ghosts. Many horrible individuals died peacefully in their beds surrounded by loved ones. Hitler had a wife so infatuated with him that she killed herself when he did. The point being, if these people weren't murdered by the millions of angry ghosts they created, then what did Aiden have to fear. A man who had only killed a dozen?

You think that makes it okay? Aiden shook his head. Tears were welling up until they overflowed and ran freely down his face. He wiped them away quickly as a woman jogger sped by. He took out a picture of his mother, and looked at her for a while. The photograph felt like it weighed a hundred pounds in his hand. He often wondered what she was like. How perfect she was? I never knew you. Aiden stood up, and walked to the edge of the river. He tossed the picture into the speeding currents. He watched as the image was carried away.

<u>A New Friend</u>

Aiden sat on the bench for a while until he heard a meow. The same old one eyed cat was following him again.

"Will you leave me alone?"

The animal stared at him blankly. Aiden sighed. He leaned down and grabbed the feline. The old cat started brushing his head against Aiden's chest. The cat was bony, and his spine looked like the crest of a mountain. Aiden kept walking. He heard his phone ring. He answered. He awkwardly maneuvered. Trying to hold the cat in one arm. It was Deirdre.

"Are you coming back?"

"Yeah, I've got a problem though."

"What problem?"

"I have a cat."

"What?"

The cat rested his head in the fold of Aiden's arm. He was falling asleep.

"I have a cat."

"A cat?"

"Yes, a cat."

Deirdre was silent for a moment.

"When did you get a cat?"

Aiden was becoming exasperated. He found it difficult to balance the animal on a single limb.

"Yes. I have a cat. Can we move on? I was at the park and he followed me. I'm sorry, I'm sorry. I really don't want to abandon it."

"That's fine, take it to the vet, and find out if there's anything wrong with it."

Aiden agreed with Deirdre's suggestion. He told her goodbye and then continued to his station wagon. Aiden wasn't sure if he had enough room. The backseat was pretty stuffed with all the junk he had cleared from the motel, and he didn't have a carrier. He put the cat in the front seat when he got back to the car. He was almost tempted to buckle the creature in. Should he be given a name? The old cat stared blankly at him with his one eye. Aiden scratched his chin. How much longer would he be with this creature? Aiden decided to name the cat George.

"You look like a George."

He scratched the cat behind his ear. Aiden shut the car door. He got into the driver's seat and started pulling out of the parking lot. Aiden only had a simple track phone, but he did have the internet. He searched for the numbers of nearby veterinarian clinics. Aiden knew of a couple a mile away from where he was. He dialed the number of one. A receptionist answered after a couple of rings. Aiden asked her when was the soonest they could schedule him was. She told him in a couple of hours. Aiden thought that was too long, but he told her that it was fine. He hung up and looked down at George.

"I bet this is the first time you've had company in a while?"

He stopped at a light, and leaned over to pet George's head one more time. The old cat purred. Aiden continued. He headed back to the motel. He knew it wasn't a place he wanted to go back to. He felt as though he had just recently escaped. He couldn't dump off a stray animal at Deirdre's place.

Aiden looked down at George. He carried George after getting out of the station wagon, and walked quickly to his room. Aiden quickly closed the door. He let George go. The cat explored his new environment. He sniffed a dirty sock that Aiden had missed in his cleaning. Aiden leaned over and picked it up. George scattered. He ran into the bathroom. There was a centipede on the floor. George pawed at it.

"You certainly are playful."

Aiden turned on the television. More news on crime.

"What the hell?"

He knew there was a lot of crime in the area, but the coverage was starting to become ridiculous. He heard a familiar name. Clarence. Aiden turned up the volume.

"A man has been gathering a group to lobby the government to change the situation on the streets, the news lady said. She interviewed a man on the street next to a church. What do you think sir? Will he be successful?"

The man was bundled up and looked like he just wanted to get home. The man shook his head. A white cloud hovered outside his mouth.

"What he's doing is dangerous. He's going to anger the wrong people."

Aiden changed the channel. He discovered an old black and white movie. The acting was stiff. He didn't think the motion picture could have been made much after the thirties. The story was about a woman trying to gain the affection of a man she sees in the library. The film was centered in a small town. Aiden loved old movies. The colorful musicals were his favorite. He would sit in splendor of Gene Kelly when he was a child.

George climbed onto the bed. He curled up in Aiden's lap. Aiden pat him on the head. The movie was coming to a close. The plot had been overly simplistic, but Aiden wasn't a critic. He enjoyed the story. There was a nice happy ending. Why couldn't all stories have a nice happy ending like that? *Maybe because life rarely has happy endings?* Aiden shook his head. He sat for a long time with George in his lap. Eventually Aiden got up. He looked at the time on his phone. He had to take George to the vet.

Aiden was surprised by the variety of creatures he saw when he got to the veterinarian clinic. As well as cats and dogs there were snakes, ferrets, and gerbils. There were even a couple of creatures Aiden didn't recognize. Aiden was holding George in his lap. He was squished between two flabby looking women. He felt like he was in the thin space between two large boulders. Aiden had been waiting for twenty minutes. He didn't understand why it was taking so long. He knew if he had been late then the doctors wouldn't have waited for him. Aiden was fidgety. He couldn't sit any longer. His leg was starting to cramp. He wanted to go out and take a walk, but he couldn't with George. Aiden heard his name called. He stood up, and walked behind a young woman in a blue uniform to a private room in the back of the clinic. Aiden thanked her for showing him the way. He sat in a cold metallic chair. More waiting followed...

He looked around. It was such a sterile location. Was this the room where beloved pets were put down? Aiden didn't have to sit so long, but coupled with how much he had been sitting already made the experience unbearable. Aiden was about to give up and leave, but then a man in a white coat opened the door.

"You are Mr. McCarthy?"

Aiden nodded. He found it jarring. Usually he didn't meet many people who called him by his last name. The veterinarian's name Aiden saw was Dr. Richards.

"Is this the guy you want me to look at?"

He pet George. The old cat purred.

"I just need to make sure he's okay. I found him in the park."

"May I pick him up?"

Aiden nodded.

Dr. Richard put George on a metal table. He began to inspect his teeth, and inspected his injured eye. The old cat wasn't as friendly this time. He started to struggle.

"It's okay," Dr. Richards cooed.

He looked back at Aiden.

"I can't see anything wrong with him. I could inspect him some more, but I really don't think he's going to live much longer."

Aiden's eyes widened.

"I thought you said he was healthy!"

The doctor nodded.

"Yes, but he's old. I'm surprised a stray like him has lived so long. My guess is he's begged food off of park visitors. There's not much I can do about the eye. He received and healed that injury a long time ago."

"So what do you think I should do?"

"Take him home."

"I can't do that!"

The doctor shrugged indifferently.

"Then you have to take him to a shelter, but to tell you the truth that would be very inhumane to an old creature like him. I'm telling you old age will take him within the year. Let him live out the remainder of his days comfortably."

Aiden was starting to become furious, but he spoke delicately, trying desperately not to raise his voice.

"Why don't you take him, hmm? You like animals. Why don't you take the cat?"

He gave Aiden a smug look.

"Sir, you found the cat."

Aiden realized the doctor was right. He sighed.

"How much does it cost to take care of a cat?"

The doctor's eye balls rolled upwards. He put his finger on his chin.

"It depends on the cat. An old one like this probably doesn't need to eat much. Make sure he doesn't go outside if you live on a busy street, but I'm guessing if he's survived this long then he should know to avoid oncoming traffic."

Aiden had nothing more to say. He didn't find the doctor helpful, but he forced himself to say thank-you. Aiden walked out with George.

"Don't die before I get to my car."

Aiden drove home quickly. George was curled into a tight ball. He was sleeping and purring. Aiden got to the motel, and George was still asleep. He carried him inside. Aiden placed him gently on the bed. George stretched his leg and yawned, but didn't wake up. Aiden went to the bathroom to take a shower. He came back out drying himself. George was still asleep. Aiden sat down on the bed. He turned on the news. He knew he shouldn't have. All the exploitation always boiled his blood, but he wanted to know how Bartley's gang was doing.

He had tried to forget his past as best he could. He wanted to make sure people like Quinn were all right. Surprisingly the news story Aiden watched wasn't about crime. It was about international trade. Local news came up next. The gang war had intensified. Three people had been killed already since Aiden had left. The reporter recalled the names, but none of them were people Aiden knew. He had seen them around, but Aiden was never very close to anyone. Quinn was a rare exception. It seemed as if the numbers were close in terms of casualties on each side.

The leader of the opposition was somebody new. The old leader had been disposed of in a bloody coup, the news lady reported. At the end of the segment the news lady promised more details as events unfolded. Aiden turned off the television. Why did he still care? He warned Quinn about the dangers. Why did it matter to him if Quinn died or not. Quinn didn't seem to care about his own fate. *He's young. It's the same reason you didn't want to kill the girl. Young people are stupid and brash. You were too, once.* Aiden shook his head. He took his phone out of his pocket. He dialed Deirdre's number.

"Hello?" Aiden smiled at the sound of her voice. "How are you doing?"

"Good. I took the cat to the vet."

"What did they say?"

"They said he'll probably die soon. He's pretty old."

"Poor thing."

"Yeah... I have two choices. I can take him to the nearest shelter. Or I could leave him here at the motel, but that would mean I couldn't move in with you right away."

There was silence on the other end. Always silence. Aiden hated waiting for answers.

"There is another option."

"What?"

"You could let him live here with us when you move. When do you intend on moving in with me?"

Aiden thought it over.

"Maybe a month?"

Alright.

"I've had animals before. I know how to take care of them. I've taken care of you."

"Funny," he replied.

She chuckled. Aiden was going to argue more, but what Deirdre was saying was what he secretly wanted. After he hung up he looked at George.

"I really shouldn't have named you."

The old cat stared back blankly. Then started brushing his head under Aiden's palm. Aiden sighed and started to pet him. Aiden left the motel. He kept George inside on the bed. George looked at him as he left.

"I'll be back."

He didn't know why he said that. George couldn't understand him, but Aiden said it anyway. He got to his car, and started driving to the nearest retail store to pick up a litter box. He hoped George wouldn't defecate all over in the time Aiden was gone. Aiden' car was still packed. He wondered if he should throw any of it out. He didn't have time to rummage through everything, but when he did he knew a lot of things would have to go. Aiden was tired of hauling everything with him. All his useless junk. Why did he keep so many things?

Aiden tried not to think about it. He got to the retail store which was only a short drive away. He could have walked, but it was snowing. Like always. He parked his car, and as he got out and nearly slipped and fell on his back. Did anybody salt? The day had been going well, but now it seemed to be taunting him. He slammed his door and continued. Aiden got into the store. It was crowded by people looking to leave as soon as they could. There was nothing like a retail store in an inner city. Even less classy of a place was a retail store in an inner city late at night.

There was a woman blatantly beating her four year old daughter. The young girl was overweight and screaming at the top of her lungs. The manager of the store stared apathetically at the situation. Aiden moaned silently. He went down the aisles searching for cat litter, and a plastic box to dump it in. He found a large bag, and he hefted it over his shoulder. Then he found a litter box, and carried it in his other free hand. He waited in line. His back was starting to ache. He wondered briefly if maybe he could still take the painkillers so long as he did it in moderation. The line moved forward. When it was Aiden's turn to pay, he dropped the heavy bag of sand, and held it so that the cashier lady could scan the bar code. She had a perky smile. Aiden gave a closed smile toward her.

"What kind of cat do you have?"

Aiden shrugged. He wasn't sure what to say. Were there different breeds of cats like different breeds of dogs? Aiden decided he was overthinking the question. She just wanted to converse.

"It's a stray. I found him yesterday at the park."

"Awe, How old is he?"

"He's old. The vet said he's probably going to die soon," Aiden said emotionlessly.

The girl stopped smiling. Why did he do that? He should have known better since his first talk with Deirdre about his bird. The girl told him the price and stopped asking him questions. Aiden gave her his money and started to leave as quickly as he could. It was still snowing when Aiden left. He put the bag of sand and the plastic cat litter box in the back seat along with all his other stuff. He didn't know why talking to other people was such a difficult task. He should be better by now. Aiden went home thinking nothing more of the day's events. George had left a present for him when he got home.

Aiden groaned, but grabbed a roll of paper towels from the bathroom. He started wiping everything up. Aiden had never smelled anything so foul before, and he had been in a car with a rotting corpse in the backseat. That was no exaggeration. It was a brown slimy liquid. No solid lumps. It had the texture of melted chocolate. Aiden couldn't get a firm grasp. It dripped when he tried to wipe it up. George looked at him from the bed. Aiden looked back at him.

"This is your mess."

Aiden finished cleaning.

He sprayed the room with an overdose of air freshener. He sat on the bed and called Deirdre.

"Are you sure you wouldn't mind me keeping him?"

"You think I'd honestly demand you take that poor animal to a shelter? Would I even be the sort of person that you'd want to date?"

"I don't want to ruin this. You're the first person I've actually cared about."

Deirdre attempted to cut in.

"Aiden…" She said.

Yet Aiden continued. He felt as though he had to get every thought out of his head or else everything would be ruined.

I love you Deirdre. You make me want to live."

Deirdre interjected once more, keeping her voice calm.

"Aiden," she said.

Aiden stopped himself. He heard Deirdre. He felt ashamed for talking over her.

"I'm sorry."

Deirdre laughed.

"You need to stop taking yourself so seriously. I don't mind the compliments, but you keep saying the same things over again. Calm down. Life will be alright."

"It never has been before."

"I know."

Sunday, January 28ᵗʰ, 46 days left

A week had gone by since Aiden's phone call with Deirdre. George had settled in at the motel. Aiden talked further with Deirdre about his planned move. Aiden wondered if it was too soon. Or maybe he was just scared. He went to church. He sat in the pew in the back. The service was over quickly. Aiden drifted in and out of consciousness. He tried to stay awake, but he hadn't been lectured for so long since elementary school. There was a long line forming to greet the pastor. He shook hands with each member and talked shortly with them. Aiden wondered if he should leave or not. He got into line. When he reached the front, the minister looked at him with surprise.

"I wasn't expecting you."

Aiden smiled at him and shook his hand.

"Things have been going well. I'm sorry about not coming last Sunday. I had car troubles."

"It's alright."

Aiden realized he was taking longer than the other people in line.

"Could we talk latter?"

"Yeah. I'm available."

"Thanks."

Aiden went outside. He sat in his car listening to music while the church regurgitated its adherents. He had bought a black leather jacket, and got rid of his windbreaker. It was comfortable enough. When the parking lot emptied Aiden went back inside the church. Richard had taken off his long robes and was in civilian clothes. He looked strange to Aiden who was used to seeing him in such extravagant clothing.

"So specifically, what have you been up to?"

Richard was sitting in a back pew. There was an open bible on his lap. He closed it and put it away. Aiden sat down next to him.

"I've been trying to get my life together."

Richard looked sympathetic.

"I guess you've been struggling a lot then?"

"No! That's the problem." He didn't mean to direct his emotion at Richard, but he was so stressed. "It's been too easy. I don't know if everything is going to collapse soon, or even worse that things might stay perfect. I would hate that. Has everything been so obtainable for so long? You mean I didn't have to suffer. I could have fixed everything long ago?"

Richard sat in silence. He wasn't sure what the appropriate thing to say was. Aiden didn't need to be comforted. He just wanted to break out. Say what was bothering him. The pressure that had been building in his chest was gone. Still a miserable feeling remained. He felt tired. Richard started to speak.

"You can help the people around you. Human beings are vile, dangerous creatures. We evolved to fight. When faced with awful circumstances we become awful, but we don't have to. Human beings can rise above our natural instincts."

"I'm sorry."

Aiden stood up. He looked one way and then the other. He wasn't sure what he was looking for. He zipped up his jacket.

"The mistakes I've made in my life are my own fault." Aiden looked down at Richard who was still sitting. "You seem like a smart man, but on this I know one thing. We all have to pay for what we've done. There's nothing I can do to fix it. I'm not that brave a man. All I can do is suffer with my guilt. That's all I've courage for."

Aiden left and he braced for the cold, but he still felt warm going outside. He got to his car and started driving. His movements were mechanic. He didn't think deliberately about anything. He was driving to the church where Clarence was holding his meeting. He would have to face the victims.

This doesn't make up for the things you've done. It's a start. The church where Clarence held his meetings was a twenty minute drive. Aiden saw the parking lot was packed when he reached his destination. Aiden took a deep breath when he pulled the keys from the ignition. Could he do this? He thought he could. His legs felt weak. He and an older woman reached the front door of the church simultaneously. He let the old woman go first. She looked devastated. Her eyes were all red like she had been crying for weeks on end. Clarence had been attracting people who had lost everything. Lost everything because of people like Aiden. He followed with trepidation behind her. He feared what he would see inside. He saw every pew in the church was filled. He felt like he was barging in on a funeral. Everyone looked miserable. There were people wiping tears from their eyes. Everyone was huddled together. They looked so fragile. Even the men looked like they were about to breakdown. Aiden sat down in the back where he hoped he would be inconspicuous. Unfortunately he sat down next to an older woman who smiled at him. Aiden wondered if he looked as uncomfortable as he felt.

"It's okay, we've all lost somebody close to us."

Aiden thanked her for her concern. He wanted this moment to be over with quickly. Yet he knew it was his own fault that he felt so terrible. He created all of these people. He saw Clarence up at the front next to who Aiden assumed was the minister of the church. The two men were sitting in separate chairs at the end of a long isle between two longs rows of pews. The minister stood up first.

"I would like to thank everyone who showed up here today. I know a lot of you have lost loved ones. We are hoping to change that. You know me. I'm Roger Foreman. There is a man more important. A man who has lost as much as anybody else…" the minister said looking back at Clarence.

The minister sat back down and Clarence stood up. Clarence looked somber. He had before when Aiden first met him, but now even more so. He was silent, as if giving a quiet prayer and then he spoke.

"I know the minister meant well, but honestly I have not suffered. Don't get me wrong, I loved my wife, but some of you have lost children. Or your children are in prison. This city is falling apart. Government corruption is one reason. We've had too many weak leaders. The bigger problem I would argue in today's world is fear. We fear each other. It seems like fear is rightfully deserved in today's world. An attack can happen at any time. I know many of you have experienced drive-by shootings in your own neighborhoods. Many bystanders can be hurt or killed in these incidents. My own wife…" Clarence stopped speaking. He rubbed his eyes with his thumb and forefinger "…We can't let this happen anymore. We can't let the government ignore us, and most importantly we can't fear each other. We need to come together."

There was a loud round of applause. Aiden clapped along with the crowd. The minister came back up to speak.

"...Now I know some of you have stories you would like to share."

Clarence introduced the first person; a middle aged man not much older than Aiden. Clarence sat back in his seat as the man he had introduced came up to stand in front of everybody. He thanked Clarence for giving him the opportunity to speak, and then he began to talk about his son.

"John died on a Tuesday afternoon." His voice was shaky. He coughed and it became flat again. "We weren't a very wealthy family. We grew up in the western part of the city. Away from the Southside, but John had friends. I used to blame them. Now I realize John made his own choices. They were bad choices. I am responsible. I must have been the one that caused him to... He bought a gun. He robbed a store. He got shot by the owner. The owner had every right. My son was a criminal. If I had been with him more, than maybe I could have prevented it. I was busy..." the man finished.

There was a round of applause. Aiden clapped too. Several other people came up to talk. None of them had as dramatic a story. They had loved ones who had been arrested or people who had been injured in muggings. At the end Clarence stood to wrap things up.

"What we have to realize is crime is not the cause of one single person or event. There is no root to all evil. There are many roots. If I had to choose one thing though I would argue the greatest contributor to the violence on the streets is power. There is too much or too little of it. We must start evening the odds by creating awareness. Write to our senators. Get people invested. Apathy is the greatest obstacle."

That and a bullet. Like the end of the preaching at Richard's church, the audience started to gather to shake hands with the minister and Clarence. Aiden waited patiently behind everybody else. He was in no rush to get to the front. He met the minister first.

"Thank-you for being here."

"You're welcome."

Aiden tried to be respectful, but it was Clarence he really wanted to see. His wish was granted.

"Well I'm glad to see you again."

Aiden nodded.

"There's been a lot of change in my life recently. I see you've gathered a large crowd for your cause."

Clarence shrugged.

"There have been a lot of devastated people. We're strong together."

"I don't know about that. You be careful."

"I don't want anybody to be hurt, but maybe it will raise awareness. Either way our goals will be met."

Aiden was going to argue against Clarence's proposed martyrdom, but realized he was making the person behind him wait so he moved on. Aiden waited in a pew and watched as people talked. Some broke out crying. Aiden thought the room was getting hotter. As the room cleared out Aiden felt better. He saw Clarence talking with one last person and together the two began to head toward the door. Aiden caught up with them.

"Hey sir, are you available? To go out I mean."

Clarence looked around as if he wasn't sure that he was the one being talked to. He looked at his watch.

"Yeah. What were you thinking? You want to grab a bite to eat?"

Aiden nodded.

That sounds good.

Clarence said goodbye to the minister, and walked outside with Aiden.

"So when did you start getting huge crowds like this?"

"It took a while. Most people were skeptical. How could I change anything? A lot of people are still skeptical. You look skeptical."

Aiden nodded.

"To be fair though I don't even believe in myself so it's kind of hard to believe in others."

Clarence gave a humorless laugh.

"I know that feeling. Hope dies quickly and has a low birth rate. Why it didn't go extinct years ago is anybody's guess. That's what I've been battling. People are so afraid of the future. Maybe that's the media. All they report on is crime. This is coming from a guy who's lost his wife. What we need to focus on now is coming together. That's the only way this city is going to get better."

Clarence suggested they go in his car. A silver boxy vehicle. Aiden got into the passenger's side. They went to a nearby diner. This time it was a familiar place. Aiden had been there once or twice in the past decade. It had existed for many years not drawing too much attention. It was like a cheap bland painting in the waiting room of a doctor's office. The food Aiden remembered wasn't spectacular and the service even less so. He didn't complain. Aiden and Clarence seated themselves in a booth in the corner. They both ordered coffee. Aiden asked for water too.

"So how have you been doing?"

"I'm moving in with my girlfriend."

Aiden realized it was the first time he had called Deirdre his girlfriend. It sounded odd to him. He was too old to have a girlfriend. Moving in with your girlfriend was something for a young man to do.

"I'm happy for you."

There was no sarcasm in Clarence's voice, but Aiden suddenly realized how alone he must be.

"Oh, I'm so sorry."

Clarence shook his head.

"Don't worry about it. I still feel her with me. It's like she's sleeping right there when I go to bed at night. You understand?"

"I understand."

Clarence nodded. Their drinks were delivered by a round waitress who didn't seem to be able to smile. She asked flatly what they would like to eat. Aiden asked for a burger. Clarence ordered fish. When she left they resumed their conversation.

"You have any idea where this movement of yours is going?"

Clarence was quiet. Contemplative. He looked out the window. His hands were folded and supporting his chin.

"I'm not sure how much longer I'm going to live. I'm old. I don't fear death. I don't fear being forgotten. Not me. I just want to do something that makes the world a better place. If I could do that then I would die happy. What would make you happy?"

Clarence asked looking at Aiden intensely. Aiden felt like he was being interrogated.

"I don't know. I want to get my life together. I want to help others, but I can't even help myself."

Clarence didn't look like he understood. He stared at Aiden blankly.

"Listen to me. Nobody knows what the answer is. You got to just do the best you can and you can't wait until you know. You have to help people with what you do know. Now."

Aiden couldn't contemplate Clarence's words. Their food came. Clarence thanked the joyless beefy woman. They ate their meals in silence. When they were done Clarence stood up. He put some money down on the table. Aiden looked up.

"Maybe we can meet some time. Not to talk about this city. I do that enough already. I just want a human conversation."

Aiden nodded. Shortly after Clarence left Aiden got out of the booth and started walking outside. It was snowing. Aiden kept walking. He saw Clarence pulled up out front. Aiden got into his car. They drove again in quiet. When they got back to the church Aiden tried to leave quickly. He hadn't disliked his time with Clarence, but there was only so much time he could spend with another human being. He still wasn't sure how he would live with Deirdre, but he would try.

"We'll meet again?"

Aiden nodded and saluted him. Clarence waved back. Aiden shut his door. He got to his station wagon. He wondered how much life the vehicle had left in it. It had been a tough winter. It rumbled, but started when Aiden turned the key. Aiden called Deirdre before pulling out of the parking lot.

"Hello?"

"What are you doing?"

"I'm watching Ben."

"Maybe you could bring him. Could we grab something to eat and go to the park?"

"That sounds good."

Aiden smiled.

"How is Ben?"

"He's sleeping."

"I guess they do that a lot?"

He never did spend much time around infants.

"Yeah."

They talked some more. Mostly trivial matters. Aiden didn't care. He was just happy to hear her voice. They talked about where to meet. Aiden suggested the pub where they first met. I don't know.

"I think we made a scene last time."

"Where would you like to go?"

"I don't mind, but let's go someplace in between."

"There is a pub up near the north end of town."

"Sounds good."

Aiden started driving after he hung up. The snow had stopped. It had left a thin crust of white. His thoughts were scattered. He kept envisioning his future. He wasn't sure what would happen. Things seemed to be going up. It wasn't stopping. Aiden's doubt was lessening. The pub was a nice enough looking place. Aiden thought it looked familiar. It had a warm exterior. Aiden hoped the inside was just as good. He looked around to see if he could find Deirdre's car. He couldn't, but there were a lot of vehicles so it wouldn't surprise him if she was there. Aiden decided to call her.

"I'm here."

"Okay. Go get a table. I'll be there soon."

Aiden hung up and walked inside. There was a sign that said *seat yourself*. Aiden saw the pub was near empty. He walked over to the window. There wasn't much of a view. Just the street, but Aiden always thought the city had a nice atmosphere come winter time. Aiden saw Deirdre searching for him, and a waitress pointed to where Aiden was sitting. She was holding Ben who was bundled up in a thick blanket.

"How has the little guy been doing?"

"He's doing well. It's cold out there. He seems to be comfortable enough. I need a new car seat though. I don't think the old one is good enough; he's getting bigger and needs the next size."

"I could help."

Deirdre smiled.

"That would be nice."

The waitress came over to take Deirdre's order. She asked for a glass of water. The waitress asked if Ben would like some crayons. Deirdre told her she thought he would sleep for the duration of their meal.

"So how have you been holding up with your new guest?"

Aiden smiled.

"George has been doing well."

"Have you had any serious issues? Are you used to taking care of an animal?"

Aiden laughed.

"I never thought I could even take care of a houseplant. I thought I would kill anything in my vicinity... But George has been doing well. I think he may have separation anxiety. He probably had more human contact when he was living alone. So far he hasn't been showing any health problems. He shat the first night I brought him home. It was a god awful mess, but nothing since then."

Deirdre laughed.

"What?"

Aiden started cracking up.

The waitress came back with Deirdre's drink. Deirdre thanked her. Aiden and Deirdre ordered their meals. Aiden wasn't very hungry, but he asked for soup. Deirdre had a salad. The waitress left.

"What have you been doing?"

"Working mostly."

Aiden grimaced.

"You shouldn't be doing that. Not with a kid."

Deirdre shrugged.

"I don't really have a choice. It's because of him that I'm working as hard as I am."

"I could help you."

Deirdre took a sip of her drink.

"I know," she said putting her glass down.

Aiden looked out the window.

"It's still snowing," he said frankly.

Deirdre reached over and put her hand on his.

"You can come over to my house tonight."

They exchanged glances and smiled at each other.

"That would be nice."

Sunday February 12th, 32 days left

Two weeks went by. George had managed to cling to life. He had an awful habit of climbing on the bed and mewing. It was a God awful shriek that made Aiden's ears bleed. Aiden thought about putting George down. Then he would open his eyes and see the old cat staring at him seeking attention. Aiden would pat George on the head and push him gently away. He figured George didn't have many days left. He hated how wrong he was.

Aiden had disposed of most of his things. Deirdre tried to help him although he had refused on a number of occasions. He needed to get rid of anything that would link him to the mob. Even though Deirdre knew he was a criminal she still didn't know Aiden had killed people, and Aiden wanted to keep things that way. He got rid of his guns first. He still had some connections from the underworld that he could use. He knew a man who could clean the weapons and make them untraceable. Turn them into scrap metal. It had been expensive. Very expensive. He had always thought moving would be so much easier, and so much cheaper. After all the money he spent he thought he was finally clean. There were problems from his past that Aiden hadn't considered.

"Who's this?"

Deirdre asked when she found a photograph of him and his mother. Aiden felt like he had just been shot. In fact Aiden would have rather been shot then experience the moment he was suffering now. He thought he had gotten rid of all the images of her.

"That would be me."

Deirdre stared at the picture more intently.

"No way! You were adorable."

Aiden smiled sheepishly.

"Who's the woman?"

Aiden's smile disappeared.

"That is my mother."

"Where is she now?"

Aiden didn't say, but when Deirdre looked at his face she knew instantly.

"I'm sorry…"

"Don't be. It happened a long time ago, but could I have the photo?"

He asked with an open hand. Deirdre gave it to him. She looked scared. Like a young child who was caught playing with something she shouldn't have. Aiden wanted their discussion to end there, but Deirdre's curiosity overcame her fear.

"How did she die?"

Aiden felt angered by her interrogation. Only he realized she hadn't meant to pry information from him. She had asked innocently enough. It was a memory he didn't want to face.

"She got into a car accident."

There was more to that sentence, but Aiden didn't want to finish it and Deirdre's curiosity had dried up. They continued going through Aiden's things. It wasn't much longer until they were finished. Deirdre had come in her own car.

"Don't you have to get back to work soon?"

Aiden realized his tone was biting. Deirdre looked hurt.

Aiden was about to apologize when Deirdre said, "yeah I better get back."

Aiden watched her go with a sinking feeling in his chest. He shook his head and went to the bathroom. He looked at himself in the mirror. He was still the brutish caveman, but there was a glimmer in his eyes. *You should turn yourself in.* I know. *You're going to hell.* I know. Aiden looked down and saw the plastic blue lighter. He picked it up before he left. Deirdre had made him a spare key. George was meowing from inside his cage.

"It's okay. You and me both want freedom."

He had gotten used to talking with George. He found it therapeutic. He wondered if his venting counted as animal cruelty. Aiden got to Deirdre's house, and started carrying his things inside. He was grateful he didn't have many heavy possessions. He had thrown out most of his things. He lacked sentiment. Deirdre had instructed him to put his things in a bedroom in the back. There was a bed in the room that Aiden sat down on. He looked around. It was empty except for his things piled together in the middle of the room. He felt a bit aimless. It was an increasingly familiar feeling. Was this really happening? All he knew was for better or for worse things were changing. Aiden thought one last trip to the old neighborhood couldn't hurt. Look at where he had come from. He wanted to see that there had truly been an improvement. Aiden stood up and walked outside. He brought George in and let him run free. Deirdre had given him permission. Ben was at daycare so George wouldn't be bothered.

Aiden got into his station wagon. The vehicle looked much better. Almost liberated. Aiden had hated driving around with so many things stuffed in the back. His thoughts were chaotic. They often were when he was trying to sleep, like ripples in a disturbed pond. Now it was the middle of the afternoon and he was awake. His internal clock was going haywire. All those naps he had taken their toll on him while he tried to sleep and bypass the ugliness of life. Sleep had been his escape. Aiden was ready to face the world. He just hoped he could survive it.

He turned on the radio. Classic rock. Sixties music. Aiden's personal favorite. They were playing a Bob Dylan cover. Aiden drove slowly observing the scenery. The old buildings. They looked nicer than he remembered. Had his life when he was a child not been as bad as he had made it up to be in his mind? Aiden didn't know. He had just been here to visit his father, and it had looked terrifying. He wasn't stopping here. Maybe it looked better because Aiden was leaving? He decided he had seen enough. He didn't know what he was looking for, but he thought he would when he saw it. People's childhoods are always exaggerated in reflection. Good or bad, but they are rarely as grand as we think they were.

Aiden just realized. He hadn't come far at all. He was stuck in the same hell he had always been in. His life was devoid of accomplishments. At best he broke even considering the good and bad things that had happened to him over the years. He knew now that he had always the chance to change. That's what he hated the most. He always had the chance, but he had never taken it. Aiden breathed deeply in and out. *You can never be happy. No matter what good things are given. You know you don't deserve any of it.* I know. Aiden turned around. He headed back to Deirdre's house. He figured he would go there and sleep. Sleep until Deirdre came back home and he could see her face. Her face which numbed the pain. She who's presence made him happy enough to live with himself. Was this finally it? The same question. Why didn't Aiden believe it yet? Things had been going so well for so long, and it still didn't seem real. *Will I ever be happy?* He asked himself. *Not until you turn yourself in.* Aiden shook his head. He knocked on Deirdre's door. She answered.

"Don't you have a key?"

Aiden smiled.

"I'm sorry, I'm still getting used to considering this my home."

He came in. He noticed it was quiet.

"Where's Ben?"

"He's still at daycare. I asked if they could watch him for another hour."

"Why?"

He noticed a mischievous twinkle in Deirdre's eyes.

"Oh."

Deirdre grabbed him by the collar, and pulled him down so she could kiss him on the lips.

"Are you ready?" She asked with a sly smile. Aiden smiled and nodded. She began to lead him to the back bedroom.

Spring Time

Their clothes were scattered on the floor beside the bed. They rested entwined under the covers. They were still breathing heavily. Deirdre's head was on Aiden's chest. She listened to his heartbeat and his breathing.

"You seem relaxed."

Aiden smiled and looked down at her. He brushed his hand through her hair.

"I always feel relaxed around you."

Deirdre laughed.

"You're getting corny."

Aiden raised an eyebrow.

"Am I?"

She smiled some more. Aiden became infatuated with her smile. He grinned with her. Deirdre looked at Aiden's chest. She saw his tattoo.

"What's that?"

Aiden looked down. He saw what she was pointing too. Ouroboros. Deirdre kept looking at him.

"I got it when I was twenty. I'm not really sure what it means. Something about cycles."

Deirdre raised an eyebrow.

"You got a tattoo and you don't know what it means?"

Aiden shrugged.

"I was stupid like that."

Deirdre poked him in the nose.

"You're still stupid."

She kissed him. She pulled her head back and Aiden could see her smiling. He smiled also. She looked at the clock on the back wall.

"Oh shit! I've got to pick up Ben."

She leapt off the bed and started to get dressed. Aiden wanted to stop her, but of course he didn't say anything. Aiden couldn't help but feel sad their moment together was coming to an end. Deirdre leaned over and kissed him right after she put on her shirt.

"I'll be back. I got to do some grocery shopping too, and maybe get a new car seat.

Aiden nodded.

"I think I'm going to catch up with old friends…"

"You're not going to be here when I come home?"

She sounded disappointed. Aiden leaned forward and kissed her.

"I'll be back."

They were both smiling again. Aiden slept a little while longer after Deirdre left. He was restless, but far from irritable. The only reason he couldn't sleep was because he felt excited. He remembered Quinn's dilemmas and realized he shouldn't feel too glad. There were plenty of people suffering. It was only luck that left Aiden out of their predicament. If he hadn't left so soon he was sure that he'd be the target of a mad man. He got up and got dressed. He felt something in his pocket. He pulled it out. It was the blue lighter. He had forgotten he had it. Aiden studied it for a minute. It would be so easy to throw it out, but Aiden put it on a brown dresser next to Deirdre's bed. Aiden walked outside. He started driving. He had a few considerations when he thought about his destination. He first called Clarence.

"Hello?"

"Hi."

"How have you been doing?"

"Good. You want to grab a bite to eat?"

The old man didn't say anything for a moment.

"Yeah, I could do that."

Aiden suggested they eat at the same diner they had first eaten at. Clarence agreed. Aiden hung up. He believed it. This life he had. He believed it now. It was happening. *Why?* I'm tired of resisting. I want to be happy.

You don't deserve happiness. Stop it! Aiden shouted inside his mind. He was gripping the steering wheel tightly. He shook his head. Just stop it already.

I want to be happy. I don't care if I don't deserve it. Who deserves anything? I know I should turn myself over to the police for the things I've done, but do you really think that would make things better? This city is a disaster. I've stopped killing. That's more than anybody else has done. If that sounds like rationalization or deflection then so be it, but I don't think it is. I'm as good as I can practically be. Aiden looked for Clarence's car when he got to the restaurant. He didn't see anything familiar so he took the keys out of the ignition and decided to walk inside and grab a booth.

The waitress took him to a table in the back corner of the restaurant. Aiden thanked her and started to think deeply about his situation. Specifically he wondered if his past would follow him. Before he wondered if a normal life was even possible, and if Bartley would let him leave. Both of those unlikely events had already happened. Aiden looked out the window. He saw Clarence's car pull into the parking spot. Aiden was glad to see him. He hoped his friend would take his mind off his worries. When Clarence came inside he was pointed in the direction where Aiden was sitting by a waitress.

Clarence was wearing a heavy looking black wool coat. He had on a flat wide brimmed hat. His attire looked weighed down by the weather, but Clarence's face still looked bright. He smiled and nodded at Aiden before he sat.

"How have you been holding up?"

"Didn't you ask me that over the phone?"

Aiden shrugged. Clarence smiled some more.

"The movement's been going well. We've got several hundred members living in the city. We've got lobby groups, and even some politicians campaigning on our behalf. I'm telling you things are looking great..."

Aiden looked out the window.

"That's not really what I meant, I still think what you're doing is dangerous, and I think you should stop for your own sake, but you told me last time you wanted to talk about something besides politics."

Clarence was silent for a while.

"I don't mind being a symbol anymore. I've reflected and realized my life as a man ended when my wife died. I breathe only now because of her memory. I don't want to see anybody else lose somebody like I lost her."

Aiden rubbed his face and brushed his hands through his hair.

"Before your wife died, what were your interests?"

"I liked gardening."

Aiden became amused.

"Is that so?"

Somehow it was unexpected to him that Clarence would have that of all hobbies.

"Why are you so shocked?"

Aiden shrugged.

"Maybe it's not you. Maybe it's this city we live in. No life can grow here except weeds."

Clarence had eyes that seemed to pry open his soul. Aiden felt vulnerable. The waitress came over. She asked them for their order. She asked for drinks. They both asked for water. Aiden told her they were ready to eat. He asked for a burger. Clarence asked for a salad. She scribbled everything down quickly on her notebook. Aiden smiled at her. She gave a fake smile back. She tried to hide her disgust. Once again Aiden had forgotten about his lack of teeth.

"So what do you like?" Clarence asked when the waitress went away. Aiden realized Clarence wasn't going to let his question go.

"I liked animals."

"Really?"

Aiden smiled and nodded. His response wasn't as awkward as he's feared. Clarence seemed to sense that there was hesitation behind Aiden's words.

"Why are you so protective of such an innocent joy? Lots of people like animals."

Aiden nodded. He was almost about to talk about his bird.

"It's just that I don't like to talk about myself at all."

"Why is that?"

Aiden started to grow irritated with the old man.

"I'd rather not talk about it."

"I never wanted to talk about my wife's death. I didn't for a long time. Bottled it up inside. I guess I was trying to protect her memory. I know you have different reasons for keeping things secret, but I know when I talked I felt better. I felt better because I helped people who had suffered similar pain as I had." He weaved his fingers between one another. "It's an interconnected web. He who helps others helps everyone. You teach."

Aiden groaned and rubbed his face.

"I really respect you Clarence and I'm happy to see you're trying to save our city, but don't give me that pass it forward shit. I've tried Clarence. I've tried."

Clarence sighed. Their drinks came before Clarence could retort. The waitress could sense the tension and quickly walked away. Aiden wanted to resolve the conflict.

"What was your wife like?"

"Tell me a bit about somebody you loved and then I'll talk."

Aiden decided it would be okay to reveal something.

"My mother kept telling me things would get better. At least that's what I remember. I keep thinking she was this wonderful person. I don't really know. Why she married the emotionless drunk that was my father I'll never know. I don't think he said two words to me on any given day. Sometimes on special occasions like my birthday I could get him to speak a whole sentence! I was always trying to get attention from him. I never succeeded. Eventually I stopped trying."

Aiden took a sip of his drink. His throat felt syrupy. Clarence took of his glasses. There were deep indentations where the rims had sat for years. He blinked a couple of times.

"Did you know your father?"

Clarence started to clean his fogged up glasses using his shirt.

"My father was a columnist for this local magazine, *Our Times*. He was a lefty, but even he knew that crime was rising in our city. It was a dilemma for him because he often campaigned against the fear mongering that was progressively getting worse in the media. He tried to tell the people that we mustn't be afraid. We should understand where this violence was coming from. Things will get better. That's what he kept saying. Things never did though. The magazine my father worked for got cancelled and he started working at whatever job he could find. He dropped dead of an ulcer at the ripe old age of thirty-five." There was no waver in his voice. He sounded very matter of fact, and his eyes were dry. "I cried for my father for years. I still feel a pain in my chest when I think about him, but I've wept as much as I can. I'm done. I've learned from the experience two things, first we must know what causes violence. It isn't television, video games, or religion. It's people. We all have free will. Poverty, mental illness, and desperation are all excellent motivators, but it is the individual who is ultimately responsible."

Aiden buried his face in his arms that rested on the table. He shook his head back and forth.

"I really, *really* don't think you know what poverty is."

He lifted his head to look at Clarence.

"Alright Aiden, I'm done."

They finished their meals quickly and quietly. Only the scraping of forks against the ceramic plates could be heard.

"I didn't mean to offend you. I have no idea what your circumstances were growing up. I was patronizing. I'm sorry... Do you like the blues?"

Aiden's eyes widened.

"Where did that come from?"

Clarence smiled.

"That was an abrupt introduction, but I've been waiting to tell you. I have tickets for a theater in the north.

A young blues artist will be performing there. I was wondering if you wanted to go."

Aiden nodded.

"That sounds good. I really love the blues."

"I'll text you when the date gets closer to the event."

"You text?"

Clarence smiled.

"Who says an old dog can't learn new tricks?"

Aiden and Clarence split the bill then left the restaurant. Aiden started to feel a little aimless when he got back into his car. He watched Clarence leave, and then he called Deirdre.

"Hello?"

Aiden smiled at the sound of her voice.

"What are you doing?"

"Eating with a friend."

"Who's that?"

You wouldn't know him. So, are you still grocery shopping?

"Yeah, I'll be home in about an hour."

"I'm going to go see another guy."

"Are you going to come out of the closet anytime soon?"

"I swear this will be the last man tonight."

Aiden said goodbye and hung up. Talking to Deirdre always made him feel better. He felt fulfilled, but he wondered why it was going to take her an hour to shop for food. Aiden never spent more than twenty minutes looking for a meal. He realized he only had to find things for himself. Deirdre was shopping for three.

Aiden knew he would have to find a job soon. There was a bulk of cash he didn't touch. He wanted to use that money to buy a new car, and maybe fix his teeth. He didn't want to do those things until he had a steady income. All those envelopes he had hidden under his mattress were now in a suitcase in Deirdre's closet. He knew he should open a bank account, but old fears are hard to overcome. He had so many things stressing him out. He wanted to talk to Richard. He loved Clarence too, but Aiden had knots in his stomach whenever he talked to the old man. He wanted to say he was sorry about the death of his wife. To say he was done with crime. Of course he couldn't. So he needed to talk to Richard. He dialed the minister's number on his phone and waited while it rung.

"Hello?"

"You must be the third person I've talked to today, which for me is a lot."

"Well that's… sad."

Aiden laughed.

"Yeah well, what are you doing?"

"I've got nothing going on. I'm free if you want to swing by the church."

"See you then."

Aiden turned the key in the ignition. The car rumbled and popped before the sounds of the engine evened out and it ran smoothly. It was cold inside the station wagon. Aiden turned on the heat. It must not have worked properly because it only gave out a low hum, even when Aiden turned the knob on to full blast. Aiden grunted and turned the heat off. He could stand to be cold for a little while.

How much longer was it anyway? Five minutes? Ten minutes? Did it matter? Aiden wasn't sure. He felt angry. His face was hot. He was grinding his teeth and twisting the leather on the steering wheel. Why was he so agitated? He took a deep breath and let the stress evaporate. He shook himself as if to loosen his body. He felt better. What had come over him? It wasn't the car. Aiden knew that much. Was he still fearful that things weren't going to work out? No. The confusion frustrated him.

Richard always tried to answer anything. Even if Aiden disagreed with Richard's responses. When he got to the church he could see the parking lot was empty except for Richard in civilian clothes standing next to a hybrid. Aiden started laughing as he parked next to Richard and got out of his station wagon. Richard gave a fake scowl.

"What's so funny?"

His hands were on his hips. Aiden shook his head.

"Nothing actually, it's perfect. I always had my suspicions that you were a hippie."

Richard rolled his eyes and the two men shook hands.

"So, what were you planning to do today?"

Aiden shrugged.

"Nothing much, maybe we could go to the park. I just ate, so I need to walk it off."

"That sounds good. As always I've got visits and a sermon to write, but I could spare a bit of time." Richard looked at his hybrid and pointed to it. "Do you want to take my hippie-mobile?"

Aiden smiled.

"Sure, why not?" Aiden realized just how cramped it was inside Richard's vehicle. "How do you drive in this thing?"

"I curl up. It gets good gas mileage."

"Does that really matter when you're ass touches your face?"

"How about you just enjoy the ride."

Aiden grumbled. The ride to the park wasn't as long as Aiden had feared. His knees cracked as he got out. He cracked his neck too.

"I'll tell you another thing. That car is silent. It's like the tiger of cars. That thing could ride up behind you and you wouldn't know it."

"Are you ready to walk yet?"

Aiden nodded, smiling foolishly.

"Have you hiked before? I mean like in some actual woods?"

Richard nodded.

"Have you?"

"Yeah... recently," he said still smiling.

He stopped. He knew he shouldn't make light of the girl's suffering.

"I was a boy scout. I never liked the boy scouts. They were too structured. I loved nature. It was peaceful to escape society. Not that I dislike the company of people. I wouldn't be doing what I do if that were the case, but it's still nice to break away sometimes."

They continued walking till the canopy of the trees blocked the sun. There wasn't as much snow on the ground where they walked. A lot of the snow that had fallen had collected on the branches of the trees.

"So, what are you afraid of Aiden?"

"What?"

He wasn't sure if Richard and he were still joking around.

"I'm getting to know you pretty well. I'm pretty sure you have a worry on your mind you want to talk about?"

To his dismay he realized Richard was very serious. Aiden laughed.

"You're right actually. I don't know what I'm trying to hide from you. I actually came here looking for your advice."

Richard smiled "... As opposed to my magnetic personality?"

Aiden smiled with him.

"I'm doing well now. I've crawled through the muck, and now I'm on top, but I'm afraid I'm going to fall."

"Why's that?"

Aiden shrugged.

"There's a reason I was on the bottom in the first place. I made a lot of mistakes. I'm a failure, Richard. I'm always going to be a failure. I just know it. I can feel it in my bones."

Richard looked at his feet as they walked. His hands were locked together behind his back.

"I've always thought it's easier to be cynical. You don't gamble. You don't put anything up. You never have to fear losing anything... but you never gain anything either. You'll never feel any sort of accomplishment. I think that's your problem, Aiden. You've never gambled anything. I think you can though. Even if you lose you just got to stand back up again. You just got to keep standing up."

"It's not just me who I'm afraid of failing. It's Deirdre and Ben."

"You're stronger than you think, Aiden. You just need guidance."

Aiden looked at Richard skeptically.

"You mean God's guidance? Are you trying to preach to me?"

Richard laughed.

"That's my job."

Aiden chuckled too.

"Fair enough, but don't you think I'm a lost cause?"

"Nobody is a lost cause in the eyes of God."

He said it quickly so it made Aiden think he had used that statement many times before.

"I've always wondered why the world is such an awful place, and don't give me that freewill bullshit. That may work for people, but what about illness, natural disasters, and permanent injuries? Why do bad things happen to people that is caused by forces outside of humanity's control?"

Richard looked disconcerted.

"Have you asked me this question before?"

"I can't remember."

Richard sighed and brushed his hand through his wispy hair. He was looking down intently at the ground.

"Maybe it just sounds familiar because other people have asked. I have trouble with that question. I could name you several theologians who've come up with adequate answers, but nothing I think that would satiate you."

Richard looked back at Aiden who was still staring intently at him. Richard almost looked frightened by Aiden's gaze.

"I guess my own conclusion is that God is testing us."

Aiden shook his head.

"If God is responsible for our suffering for whatever reason; fuck him."

Aiden spat on the ground. The path they had been walking on broke out into a clearing. There was a dead meadow on either side. Richard was looking at the blue sky. It was cloudy, but the light shined through the grey sheet. Aiden was staring far away into the horizon with tired eyes. He felt hypnotized. Aiden could hear an incessant buzzing sound in his ear. He shook his head. The buzzing sound persisted at a lower pitch.

"Somebody much smarter than me once philosophized- I can understand when people look at the ground and say there is no God, but how can you say the same thing when you look to the sky?" Richard turned to face Aiden. "You can still see beauty in the world if you look hard."

Aiden thought of Deirdre.

"I see beauty."

"Do you see beauty in yourself? You're a good person, Aiden."

"I'm gone. There's nothing left of me. I only keep going out of selfishness."

Aiden still felt woozy; a similar feeling to drunkenness. What was it? He stared at Richard. He thought he might slur his words.

"I look in the mirror and I see blackness. I see a deep void. There is nothing for me. I'm going to hell. I can't stop it. I can only accept it. You see good in me because you don't know what I've done. I'm not even a human being. I'm an animal," Aiden said through clenched teeth.

Richard put his hand on Aiden's shoulder.

"Let's go." As they turned around, Richard looked at the ground and saw a flower. "Spring time will be here soon."

<u>Facing fear</u>

Aiden said his goodbyes to Richard. The answers he had sought were nowhere. Maybe there was a chaos outside of God's control. Maybe God wasn't all powerful. Maybe God was dead. Aiden stopped hypothesizing. He drove home eager to meet Deirdre. Aiden stopped to get gas. The station attendant filled his tank. He paid through his rolled down window. Aiden didn't acknowledge the man. He handed his money without looking. He hadn't meant to be rude, but he was trapped inside his own head. His worries besieged him.

"Your tank's full," the attendant said.

"Keep the change."

It was only later Aiden realized he had underpaid the man by fifty-five cents. He pulled over and started weeping. Not for the fifty-five cents. He wept because of confusion. He didn't know if he should feel happy or sad. Or scared. All he knew was things were changing. He stopped crying. He was a grown man. He wiped some green slime that had run out of his nose. It was time to become more civilized. Aiden did a Pierce Bronsan look in the rear view mirror. He smiled some more. He was about as regal as a rat. He started up the car and continued driving. Somehow he knew he'd make it. He got to Deirdre's house not long before she pulled into the driveway.

"Good timing," he said getting out of the car.

Deirdre was taking Ben out of his car seat. Aiden walked over to help her with the groceries.

"The new car seat is in the back. Could you get that for me?"

"Sure."

Aiden was already holding five full bags. He carried what he already had inside the house. He put the bags on the table and started putting away two milk jugs and a frozen dinner. Deirdre came in soon after. She was carrying a sleeping Ben.

"You didn't get the car seat?"

"Well I had to get the groceries."

His tone was slightly deeper than usual. He sighed. He could feel his bones ache. His head was throbbing.

"Yes, but you could have carried in the car seat too."

Her voice was slightly higher than usual. Aiden was starting to breathe faster. He was starting to sweat. He could feel pains in his chest.

"Well I was putting away the groceries first."

You could have done that after you carried in the car seat.

"Couldn't you have done that?"

Aiden felt a tingling sensation climbing its way up his spine.

"I had Ben."

"Yes, and I'm sure all five pounds of him weighs you down!"

Aiden was gritting his teeth; why was he feeling so ill?

"I've been working all day!"

Aiden put his hands up.

"I'm done."

He walked past her and out the door. He saw that she was parked behind him.

"Could you move your car?"

Aiden knew things couldn't work out. Deirdre put Ben in his crib and stormed out of the house with her keys in her hand. She got into the car and proceeded to pull away from the back of Aiden's station wagon. Aiden got into his vehicle. Yes, he was happy. He realized was what he had wanted all along. No more worrying. It was just him. Alone again. He put the stick in reverse and backed out as quickly as he could. He had figured in his mind that he would speed away without looking back. Well... Maybe one look couldn't hurt. He could see Deirdre scowling at him in his rearview mirror. He laughed. Her scowl grew meaner.

He put his foot on the accelerator. What he hadn't predicted which in hindsight was obvious, was that Aiden's emotions were more powerful than his junky car. He only managed to get a few feet before he heard a pop and smoke started billowing out of the engine. Aiden was thrust forward. His airbags had failed to deploy. Damn. His head had hit the steering wheel. He rubbed his forehead. That's going to bruise. He looked outside and he could see Deirdre rushing to his window. Aiden was still holding his head which had a large open gash.

"Are you okay?"

Aiden nodded.

"Idiot! What the hell is wrong with you?"

"What's wrong with me? You flipped out because I didn't get the car seat."

Deirdre bit her bottom lip. She nodded and looked down at her feet.

"Yeah, I might have overreacted."

Aiden laughed.

"I can't deal with explosive people. I need to know what set you off. If something like that makes you crazy then what's going to happen when we experience real problems?"

Deirdre nodded.

"You're right, you're right. You just have to understand though…" she continued with watery eyes, "I've been betrayed so many times. When you moved in it's been building up inside me. I keep expecting you to be gone any minute. At some point I just decided to get it over with."

Aiden nodded.

"You were right to fear me leaving you. I thought I might leave you, but I wanted to make this work. We both need help."

"Are you alright?"

Aiden saw that an onlooker came to check up on them. Aiden nodded.

"I called the police, they should be here soon."

"Thank-you."

Aiden looked at Deirdre.

"I guess we better get out of the road."

Deirdre nodded. Aiden got out of the car and started to push the station wagon from behind. His objective was to get it as close to the curb as possible. Deirdre started to help him. The station wagon was heavier than it looked. When they were done they both collapsed next to each-other. They were breathing heavily. I think I'm going to run inside and grab us both a couple of beers.

"Not me."

Deirdre looked at him.

"You sure?"

Aiden nodded. His back was on fire. He wasn't taking pain killers anymore. Aiden dabbed his forehead with the bottom part of his shirt. He was still breathing hard. Jesus. It was the only word he managed to get out. He wondered about his heart. Is that how he would die? He hoped not. Then again, he wasn't sure how he wanted to go. Deirdre came back.

"I got you water."

Aiden thanked her. He was glad to have something to drink. Aiden could hear sirens in the distance. He wondered how awkward it would be if he met an officer that used to work for Bartley. After a satisfying swig, Deirdre gasped and looked at Aiden.

"I really hated sobriety when I was pregnant with Ben. I'd never be able to scold my kids if I had any."

Deirdre thought for a moment.

"What's the saying…? Do as I say, not as I do?"

Aiden smiled and took another sip of his water.

"People are hypocrites."

Aiden's ear pricked up. The sound of the sirens had grown louder.

"I used to fear the cops growing up."

Deirdre lowered her head and started to cry. Aiden put his arms around her shoulders. He would have cried with her, but his eyes were dry. Instead he just let her weep into his chest. He could see the patrol car. Deirdre sniffled. She wiped her eyes before the officer emerged from the vehicle. Aiden was thankful. He didn't know him. He was a very serious looking individual. Aiden could tell he was a man from the south, but there were a lot of police in the south. Not all of them were corrupt, but they never stuck their noses in any business they didn't belong. He looked at Deirdre and Aiden with sympathy.

"So it seems you two have had a little trouble, he said with his hands on his hips." He managed to sound both caring and authoritative at the same time. Aiden nodded at the officer's rhetorical question. "Well, that's no trouble. I'll take some statements and block off the road till that thing is off the street."

Aiden looked at his car. The side mirror was cracked and bent. It dangled by a single plastic thread before coming loose and smashing on the ground.

"Fair enough."

Aiden talked longer with the officer about insurance. He told the officer that he had been experiencing car trouble, and that he had intended on buying a new vehicle. No citations were given. The officer said nobody was to blame. He suggested they call a Tow Truck. Deirdre offered to make the phone call. Aiden felt embarrassed that he was causing so much trouble for her.

They spent a long time waiting. Aiden hated waiting. He kept playing mental games with himself. He looked around the neighborhood and then closed his eyes and tried to see if he could remember any of the scenery. Deirdre's house was one home in a long row adjacent to a duplicate row. Each house was built the same, except that each house was a different color. Deirdre's house was blue. The road was calm. There were people outside looking at the wreckage. There was a tough looking bald man in a leather jacket. He could have been a biker. Or a poser. There were a couple of kids playing in somebody's yard. They were about seven or eight, and they were fencing with sticks. They were both boys. Both white. And it was snowing.

The game was getting boring. Aiden opened his eyes. He saw the police officer walking over to him. Deirdre was making a phone call. She had finished and was walking back over to Aiden. The officer still had his hands on his hips. Aiden wondered with amusement if the officer could stand any other way. His chest was puffed out and his chin was held up high.

"When the tow truck comes, I think you can relax and go back into your home. I would suggest finding your next car from a reputable owner."

Police officers were one of the few men who could afford to be condescending. Aiden realized why he always had trouble with the law. He nodded, and thanked the officer for his services. Aiden spat when the officer turned around. Deirdre walked up to him, and Aiden pretended to be civil.

"I called the tow truck company; they'll be here in fifteen minutes."

Aiden nodded and kissed her.

"Thank you."

They walked back to Deirdre's house and sat on her front porch. Many of the onlookers had gone back inside their own homes. Aiden could easily imagine himself living here. Did he deserve it?

"Do you think you could ever forgive your father?"

Deirdre stopped and looked at her feet. She tucked a black stand of hair behind her ear.

"If he was truly sorry, then yes… but I don't think he ever was."

Aiden nodded as if he understood.

"Did he ever apologize?"

Deirdre nodded.

"Yes, but that doesn't make him sorry."

"What would?"

"If he had turned himself in willingly."

Aiden looked up at the sky.

"We'd better go inside, it's snowing."

They sat on the couch while Aiden looked out the window. He wasn't sure when the tow truck would arrive. It could be any minute, but the weather was getting worse. Deirdre sat down on the couch next to him.

"So what was your father like?"

Aiden gave an annoyed look.

"If you don't mind me asking."

Aiden sighed. He had asked her about her father.

"He wasn't much of anything. He sat on his ass all day and drank. It left me plenty of time to go around ruining my life."

"Where was your mother?"

Another question that stung. Aiden knew she hadn't meant to be offensive, but nonetheless she prevailed.

"She was dead."

"I'm sorry."

Aiden shrugged.

"I was too young for the incident to impact me. My father had his own way of dealing with things."

"Is your father dead too?"

"Last time I talked to him he was in a wheelchair."

Deirdre was quiet.

"My father's in prison. I didn't talk to him for a long time either. I eventually went to see him. I just wanted to prove to myself that I could look at him without hatred."

"Did you?"

Deirdre shook her head.

"I couldn't." Aiden had expected as much. He put his hand over hers. She looked at him. He thought she was going to kiss him. "I went back. I listened to him, and I realized I had to forgive him. Not because he apologized, but because I knew he couldn't help himself. There was something wrong with his brain."

Aiden thought of his own father. All that work he had done to prove he had changed.

"The problem with my father is that he changed too late."

"You mean he changed?"

Aiden nodded.

"You have to forgive him."

"I can't."

"Why not?"

Aiden sighed. He looked into her eyes. He could see how hopeful they were

"...Please don't. I don't tell you how to deal with your problems, so could extend me the same favor?"

Deirdre looked down. She appeared bashful.

"I'm sorry. I still think you should talk to him though."

Aiden looked out the window.

"Maybe..."

Deirdre was about to say something else, but then the tow truck arrived.

"Let's go out."

The tow truck driver was a short man with a floppy hat and a cigar sticking out the side of his mouth. He wore fingerless gloves and a vest. He left his flabby arms bare in the cold. On his right shoulder he had the letters VIP tattooed. Aiden gave the man a funny look when he saw him. The man sort of growled back. He had short black curly hair and the face of a bull dog. He was furiously scribbling something down on a piece of paper. When he was done he stuck the pencil behind his ear. Aiden looked around. He wondered if the company had sent the right guy. He handed the paper over to Deirdre. More like shoved it. Aiden was furious. He thought about saying something, but he saw Deirdre wasn't angry and he thought she might be if he made a scene.

"Sign here," the man demanded.

The moment was short lived. Deirdre handed the paper back, and he got into his truck. He had already hooked the station wagon to the back. As he drove off Aiden felt a little happier.

"If I was twenty years younger..."

"What?"

Aiden shook his head.

"Nothing, let's go inside."

Deirdre smiled.

"What?"

Deirdre rolled her eyes.

"You were about to pick a fight."

She pointed a finger at him. Aiden pretended to be offended.

"I most certainly was not!"

Deirdre laughed. Aiden smiled with her. He put his arm around her shoulder and they kissed.

"I don't want to fight anymore."

When they got inside Deirdre had stopped, but Aiden kept walking and soon found himself alone. He turned around to see Deirdre looking at him with her arms folded. He looked at her for a moment not sure what he had done wrong. Deirdre didn't leave him in suspense.

"You should see your father."

Aiden groaned.

"Not this again, I thought we were done?"

Deirdre was still staring at him seriously.

"What?"

Deirdre's face softened.

"I know you had your problems." Aiden laughed at her understatement. He started to pace. He was going to walk away. He decided to at least hear her out. "I know how difficult it is, and I'm not patronizing you."

"You're not?"

She shook her head.

"No, you know what I've been through."

Aiden groaned some more and pulled his hair. He knew she was right. Aiden sighed. He looked at her. He saw her smiling because she knew she had won.

Sunday February 19th, 25 days left

A week had come and gone since the accident. Deirdre pushed Aiden to visit his father. She never forgot, which Aiden had a small hope she might. They'd paid off the debts from Aiden's car. He was glad he had put that mess behind him. Aiden was drinking coffee and reading the newspaper in the kitchen when Deirdre woke up. Aiden saw Deirdre and he put the newspaper down.

"How did you sleep Honey Buns?"

"Fuck off."

Deirdre wasn't a morning person. Her black hair stood on end like somebody had run a balloon over her head, and her eyes had dark circles under them. It took several hours before she acted human. It didn't stop Aiden from teasing her. She got some coffee and sat down at the kitchen table next to Aiden.

"We are going to see your father today."

"You are a monster in the morning."

Deirdre smiled. She was still in her bathrobe and slippers. Light flooded into the kitchen. Aiden could feel a layer of sunshine on his skin. He was feeling good. He closed his eyes. He thought he might be able to take a nap. Deirdre interrupted his thoughts.

"Could you make me breakfast?"

Aiden moaned and rubbed his face. She gave a large exaggerated pout.

"You're not that cute."

"Yes I am."

He sighed and went to the fridge. There were eggs, cheese, and milk.

"You want an omelet?"

Deirdre shook her head. Her hair drifted from side to side. She looked like a little girl.

"Do you know how infuriating you are?"

She smiled and pointed to the cupboard.

"I want pancakes."

Aiden sighed and opened the small wooden door. He found the pancake mix behind a can of tomato soup. He turned on the stove. Aiden had never been very good at cooking. He hadn't made pancakes since he couldn't remember when. He hadn't forgotten everything. He had seen enough cooking shows to know how it was done.

"They may be a tad crunchy, he warned as he slid the flapjack onto a plate."

Deirdre only grimaced slightly.

"You better eat that."

Deirdre sighed. Aiden sat down across from her.

"Can you tell me what your father was like?" She asked after gnawing on Aiden's leathery pancake.

Aiden did not want to have this conversation, but it was unavoidable.

"He wasn't much of anything."

Deirdre seemed disappointed.

"Can you at least try? I could find some good in my father."

Aiden shook his head.

"I'm not trying to argue with you, my father wasn't there for me when I needed him. He lost a wife. I get it. I lost my mother. What I hadn't expected was that I'd lose my father too. I don't hate him. I never loved him in the first place."

"You can't remember one good thing?"

Aiden shook his head.

"Try."

Aiden sighed. He thought back. He smiled.

"I remember one thing. He used to always give me money. Mostly so I would go away so he could mope. I remember one time though, he stopped me. I guess maybe he wasn't drunk enough. He cried for a while and told me to be strong. He was never physically abusive. I guess I can count that as a plus."

"Let's go see him. He can't be that bad."

Aiden laughed.

"You want to bet?"

Deirdre ignored him and took her plate to the sink.

"You're not going to finish your pancake?"

She looked back and smiled.

"I'll make you breakfast one of these days, and it'll taste a hell of a lot better."

"Well... you *are* a woman."

Deirdre put her plate down and walked over to Aiden. She was about to smack him. Aiden caught her wrist. She struggled. Aiden pulled her down so that she sat on his lap. She turned her head around to look at him. Aiden stole a kiss. She raised an eyebrow like she was about to make a sly remark.

"I'm going to go get dressed."

Aiden let her go and watched as she walked away. Aiden picked up the newspaper he'd been reading. The Night Horses had perpetrated several attacks over the past month. They started out small. Running protection rings, dog fighting games, and drug smuggling. They went under the radar of men like Bartley. He hadn't thought they would ever threaten him. Then the paper said Bartley, the *alleged* crime boss was missing since the Night Horses had taken control of the streets. Aiden remembered Quinn's story. He pushed the newspaper away. He heard Deirdre.

"Are you ready to go?"

Aiden looked down at himself. He was wearing a white polo shirt and some tan slacks. He had expected to go job searching sometime later in the day.

"I might be overdressed."

"You'll be fine."

Deirdre came out and Aiden looked at her. She wore blue jeans, boots with short heels, and a purple blousy shirt.

"I think you might be a little overdressed too."

"I want to look nice when I meet your father."

She did an exaggerated curtsey.

He doesn't deserve any attention.

"Deirdre put her hands on her hips."

"Then why are we going?"

"Because you're Making ME!"

Aiden hadn't meant to yell at her, but his anger and anxiety were boiling over. Deirdre didn't mind. She walked over and sat next to Aiden at the table she put her arm around him and rested her chin on his shoulder. Her mouth was close to his ear. He could hear her breathing.

"Try, for me…"

Aiden tilted his head so he could look at her brown eyes.

"Stop it!" He moaned and shook her off. "I'll go, and I'll try, but enough of the sappy crap. I'm not going to fall for it."

She laughed. It was light and optimistic.

"So you say your father couldn't help himself. That's why you forgave him?" Deirdre nodded. Aiden continued. "I don't know what my mother was like. She died when I was ten. My memory of my father before my mother died is vague. I know my mother's death destroyed him, but he had a son to take care of."

He looked at Deirdre. He thought she might understand.

"Aren't there some things you could have done to make your life better?"

"I never had kids or a wife. I stopped doing all the bad things as soon as I met you." Deirdre gave him a skeptical look. Aiden was a little annoyed. "I did!"

Deirdre sighed.

"Then do it so you can move on."

"I have moved on."

Deirdre shook her head. Aiden was about to say something else, but Deirdre spoke before him. She put up a finger to stop him from talking.

"You've suppressed your emotions. That's not the same thing as moving on. Now can you please get your shoes on? I feel like I'm talking to a child."

"Whatever."

They walked out the door a couple minutes later. Aiden had grabbed his black leather jacket. He followed her to her car. Aiden got into the passenger seat. Deirdre turned on the radio. Aiden looked out the window. He sighed. He wished the day would go fast. Deirdre put her hand on his knee.

"It will be over soon."

Aiden smiled at her and went back to looking out the window. He couldn't verbalize his thoughts. It was a mixture of fear and panic, but also something light. He didn't know what it was. It only existed because Deirdre was with him. It was an inner strength. Aiden felt like he would survive. As they rode it started snowing. Aiden gave Deirdre the directions to his childhood home. He wondered how she would perceive it. She looked curious.

"This actually doesn't look as terrible as I had imagined."

"No?"

Deirdre shook her head.

"I thought I'd hear gun shots and sirens as soon as I was within a mile of this block. This looks like it used to be a nice place once."

"It was," Aiden admitted, still looking out the window. The neighborhood was always close to collapsing, but the people were tight knit. I knew everyone. They looked out for each-other.

"What happened?"

They passed a shutdown shoe factory.

"We were forgotten."

Aiden thought about politicians who were elected on false promises. They visited his neighborhood when he was young. He could still remember one well-dressed man volunteering at a soup kitchen. Aiden remembered how strange the experience was. How such a well-dressed man was attempting to interact with slum folk. He was too young to understand manipulation. He had been at the soup kitchen with another boy. They had been brought by a church lady to help volunteer. Even though they were as poor as anybody else.

Only the poor help the poor. The wealthy merely pretend. Taken as a percentage Aiden knew a minimum wage earner giving ten dollars to a Santa ringing a bell was worth more than a rich man donating half a million dollars. It was all publicity. When the reporters had left, Aiden saw the politician become less friendly. By the end of the hour he had given up. Aiden, who still had school work to do, worked well until they end of the night. He didn't scorn the politician. He scorned the church lady who had forced him to come.

"That's it."

Aiden pointed to his father's house. Deirdre parked across the street.

"I'm going to come in with you. Make sure you actually *talk*."

Aiden was secretly glad. He would have feared to go alone. He got out of the car and Deirdre waited till he was near the front door before she got out. He started knocking. It seemed to be taking forever. Deirdre came up behind him. She noticed it was taking a while.

"You think he may not be home?"

Aiden chuckled.

"He's in a wheel chair."

He looked to his right. There was an elderly woman shoveling her driveway. Excuse me, miss? She stopped and stabbed her shovel into the ground. She looked slightly crazy. She wore a red snow jacket with the hood up. Her frilled white hair snuck out in places, and her eyes were wide open and intense. Aiden took a small step back. He felt like a character in a horror movie after the villain had just popped out.

"Yes?"

Her voice was shrill.

Aiden cringed. He gulped a little.

"Do you know where the man who lives here is?"

"They took him to the hospital."

"What?"

"They took him to the hospital."

Aiden couldn't think. His mind was on fire. He started to panic. He ran down the steps and tapped Deirdre on the arm. He could see she was as shocked as he was.

"Where are we going?"

"St. Luke's is the nearest hospital."

Deirdre didn't ask any more questions. She didn't even complain when she got into the passenger's seat of her car. Aiden drove quickly. Deirdre tried to remind him to slow down, but she noticed Aiden had tears pricking at the corners of his eyes. When they got to the hospital Aiden was hyperventilating. Sweat was pouring down his face. He looked frantically for a parking space. They discovered one on the far end of the lot.

Deirdre reached over and put her hand over Aiden's as he gripped the steering wheel tightly.

"It'll be okay," she said soothingly.

Aiden looked at her. He wiped his eyes with his thumb.

"Let's go."

She stayed calm. Aiden got out. Deirdre raced over and grabbed his hand. They walked together. Aiden was still worried, but his emotions cooled with Deirdre by his side. Aiden suddenly had a serious migraine when he got indoors. Why were the lights so bright? Deirdre started to rub his back.

"Come on."

Her voice wasn't a guarantee that things would be alright, but it suggested Aiden would be able to handle the news, no matter what it was. Aiden looked at the receptionist. She was a plump lady. Short dark hair, small in stature, and Aiden stood over her. He was petrified. Aiden silently prayed. *You know I never had a relationship the man. I can't explain it either. I'm not asking for money, fame, or hell... to even get my life together. I just want a fond memory with my father.* Deirdre realized Aiden had trouble forming the words in his mouth. So she spoke.

"Do you have a man by the name of Harris McGrath?"

The receptionist looked at them sympathetically. She could easily read the emotion etched on Aiden's terrified face.

"I'll check."

She bit her bottom lip, and quickly typed on her computer. Her eyes went back and forth as she read something on her screen. She bit her lip even more.

"What is it?"

Deirdre started to sound panicked. The softness of her voice had hardened. Aiden waited in agony. His mind began to numb. He listened to a clock tick on the back wall. A fly was buzzing somewhere. People were chatting.

"I'll see you tomorrow, Susan," he heard a man say.

"Alright," a woman replied, "just make sure you drive carefully. The roads are terrible. It's still snowing."

"It always is."

"He's dead."

Aiden's mind became focused again. He didn't know what to say.

"What?" Deirdre spoke for him.

"I'm sorry..." the receptionist said.

Aiden stumbled backwards. It couldn't have happened. Aiden knew it couldn't have, except that it did. He managed with Deirdre's guidance to sit down without falling. Aiden kept shaking his head back and forth. He tried talking, but he wasn't saying anything. Deirdre put her arms around him. Aiden was finally able to speak. Deirdre's embrace somehow unclogged his mind.

"I've tried. I keep trying. I've failed. Nothing matters."

"Everything matters." Deirdre whispered.

Aiden didn't cry. Partly out of shock. Partly because he had cried too much in his life. He was all dried up inside. Today was the last day.

"Everything matters."

Somehow Deirdre's words got into his head. Aiden nodded. She walked him outside, back to the red truck.

"Can you wait here? I'm going to check on something."

Aiden nodded. He stared out the window and up at the white sheet of sky. The snow collected on the windshield. The windows fogged up; Aiden drew a cross with his finger. He looked at it. He admired it. He laughed. Then he wiped the image away with his sleeve. There really isn't anything out there? Deirdre came back sooner than expected. She sat in the driver's seat without driving. She was staring straight ahead, back into the hospital.

"They say he died quickly. They used a lot of medical jargon. I didn't understand. The state cremated him. They gave me a number to contact. We can still collect the ashes."

Aiden heard her. He nodded. He looked up. Deirdre stared at him. She thought he was about to say something. Aiden thought he was about to say something

"…Let's go."

Deirdre pulled out of the parking lot.

"He wasn't all bad." Deirdre was looking at him, but Aiden wasn't really talking to her. He smiled and laughed. "I remember he had me on his lap once. We were watching television. It was a cowboy movie. As the cowboy rode his horse my father would bounce me up and down on his knee. I'd pretend to be the hero in the movie." Aiden stopped smiling. "That was when my mother was alive. Aiden shook his head. I don't know if any of that stuff actually happened. I was too young, but maybe I'm just trying to make believe. I'm too old to pretend that things like that existed or can exist. It's better to be certain. I can be certain there is nothing left. When you're gone, you're gone."

"Stop saying that."

"What?"

He wasn't aware that Deirdre had been listening. He still thought he was talking inside his own mind.

"I'm with you Aiden."

He knew she was right, and yet he didn't want to listen. They went back to their house. Their house. Their house. Aiden kept repeating. It was starting to sound right. Aiden's chest didn't feel so tight. When they pulled in the driveway Aiden felt like he could breathe again.

"Do you want me to call?"

Aiden slowly turned his head to her. He was seriously contemplating her question.

"No, I'll do it."

They both walked to the door. Deidre tried to help him.

"I can walk," Aiden said throwing her arms off. He felt bad. Deirdre looked hurt. "I'm sorry. I'm actually feeling... I just. I don't know. Whenever I think things are going good I get thrown a curveball. I can't take it anymore."

Deirdre hesitantly put her arm on his shoulder.

"Let's go inside."

Aiden sat down on the couch while Deirdre went to the kitchen. She handed him the number the receptionist had given them. Aiden took out his cell phone. He dialed each digit slowly. He pushed himself to complete the task. He listened patiently while it rang. Deirdre came back out with a glass of water in her hand. She sat next to Aiden on the couch. Hello? A voice answered on the phone. Deirdre handed him the glass of water. Aiden spent the next half hour on the phone giving information, and learning more about his father's remains. They talked about his will. There wasn't much. The most important thing Aiden wanted to know was if he could receive his father's ashes.

He asked when he could get them. Aiden hung up the phone.

"What do you think you'll do?"

"I don't know. I've got to do some recollecting. I need to know something good happened between me and him." Deirdre started to rub Aiden's back. He felt good when she touched him. In spite of the day. Aiden kissed her. "I'm going to go for a walk."

Aiden stood up.

"I'll make dinner for you when you come back if you're still hungry."

Aiden nodded.

"That would be nice."

He opened the door and stepped out. He was greeted by the cold. He hadn't felt a chill in a long time. It felt good. It was snowing. He looked around. Some cars drove by on Deirdre's quiet street. There were a few people out, but the neighborhood wasn't overpopulated. Aiden smiled. Something had been lifted off of him. He continued down the steps and walked down the sidewalk. It was quiet. There was always a hush in wintertime, even in the city after the snow fell. Aiden thought days like these were too rare. He was able to think. He could smell the freezing air. He drank it through his nose and felt it slide down his throat. Aiden didn't know where the conclusion of his trip would be. He decided it wasn't important.

I loved you dad. You were a flawed man, but so am I. I don't know why I couldn't get through to you. I'm thinking loving a rock might have been easier. Aiden laughed aloud. He wiped his nose. *Maybe I loved the idea of you, like I loved the idea of mom. Truth is I really don't know.* Aiden stopped at a light. He supposed it was a good time to turn around. He shook his head as snow piled on top of his hair. He smiled some more. He was walking home.

Tuesday February 21st, 25 days left

Two days passed before a man delivered his father's ashes. Aiden signed the paperwork and thanked the man. He looked at the pinewood box. It was nice.

"Are you going to keep it?"

Aiden turned around. Deirdre had been washing dishes. Aiden shook his head.

"Now?"

"Yeah, might as well."

Deirdre got her keys.

"You want to drive?"

"That's okay."

They got into Deirdre's truck.

"Where did you want to go?"

"The park."

Aiden wondered how busy the park would be. He hoped to have some solitary time. It was midday on Wednesday. He couldn't imagine there would be that many people. He held the box in his lap. He had been to the park before, he reassured himself. It wasn't always busy. They parked and Aiden saw there were only a couple of vehicles besides their own. Deirdre got out first, and Aiden took a deep breath. He opened his door. Deirdre smiled at him. Aiden felt reassured. They began following the cement path that paralleled the river. They came to the spot.

"It's a nice place," Deirdre said, but her real question was evident although it had not been asked. Why had Aiden chosen this spot? Aiden wasn't sure what to say.

"I used to come here when I was a kid. I would skip rocks in this river. It was the place I went to when my mother died. I came here when my father had drunk himself to sleep. The river doesn't look any different than it did when I was a kid." Deirdre listened patiently. "They have photographs of the river from a hundred years ago. It looks the same. A hundred years from now it will too." He opened the pinewood box. He knelt by the water's edge. His foot sank in the mud. "Shit." He quickly opened the box and dumped the ashes into the fast moving stream. He turned around. Deirdre gave Aiden a hand and he crawled back up onto the cement path. He looked one direction and then another. He made sure they were alone. He watched his father's ashes drift away from him. "I had a speech prepared, Aiden said with a laugh." Deirdre smiled and put her arm around his shoulders. Aiden had hunkered low. He looked like a hunchback. His hands were kept tightly at his sides. The wind blew. His hair went in all directions. The different wild black strands were dancing on his head. "I've feel like I've been standing still my whole life. The world passed me by. I thought I was content being where I was..." He paused.

"Go on," Deirdre urged.

Aiden looked again nervously about.

"Nobody's here."

Aiden nodded. His heart was beating fast.

"I'm moving on, dad. I know it was something you could never do. I never understood why. Now I do. You had a kid though. You had responsibilities. I never wanted any because I knew..." Aiden said, and he stopped again.

"Do you want to continue?"

Aiden shook his head.

"I'm done." He looked at the bench behind them. "I want to sit down."

Deirdre and he sat together. They watched the river flow. There wasn't as much ice in the water this time. Spring time was coming. They waited for a long time. Nobody passed. Deirdre and Aiden stood up. They were walking back when Deirdre stopped. She saw a white flower.

"Should I cut it?"

"No, let it grow."

Thursday February 22nd, 20 days left

"I'm wondering... is God mute or deaf? I'd really love to hear your explanations."

Aiden was sitting at a restaurant with Richard. They sat near a window that overlooked a busy street. Aiden had been here before, but it had been two days since he had been to the park. He could see the sun and there was still snow on the ground, but the weatherman promised more snow to come; one last blizzard before spring bliss. Richard had stiffened at Aiden's question. Richard knew why Aiden wanted to see him. He had told Richard his father had died, and Richard took time to deal with the problem, but he still didn't think he was prepared. He looked out the window and paused, but it wasn't a diversion. He was trying to think.

"Some people say God is a clockmaker. They say he made the world then sat back and watched as everything unfolded..."

"I don't care what other people say. I want to know what *you* think."

Richard scratched the back of his neck.

"I don't know, Aiden."

"I figured."

Richard sighed. He rubbed his face.

"I haven't the answer, but I got as many questions as you do... Sometimes I think I may have chosen the wrong profession... You're shutting people out. I think this may be the end of the road for us."

...because you can't answer what I'm asking.

Richard stood up, and he straightened his black wool coat. He put on his floppy wide brimmed grey hat.

"You're not looking for an answer, Aiden."

Richard laid some money down on the table and continued walking out the door. Aiden sat for a moment wondering. He put his face down on the table. He didn't know if it was his fault. Why didn't he have faith? How do you earn it? Aiden looked up. He wondered where the waitress was. He saw her over at another table, but he decided he would wait patiently for her to come. He looked at the television. He wondered what was happening on the streets. It had been a struggle for him. He was always afraid of what he might hear. So far as he knew Quinn was still alive. Aiden decided to head home. Deirdre was holding Ben when he walked through the door.

"Yes?"

Aiden breathed again. He walked over and knelt by her side and kissed her.

"What's up with you?"

He kissed her again.

"Get over yourself."

Deirdre laughed and pushed him away.

"Shit… I have to be at work in fifteen minutes."

Aiden nodded and said goodbye as she walked out the door. Aiden looked at Ben who stared back at him wide-eyed. He had thin black hair and chestnut eyes. Aiden smiled at him.

"You're not so bad, are you?"

Aiden walked over and sat next to the toddler on the couch. Ben followed Aiden with his eyes. He had a serious face for somebody so young, but Aiden poked Ben in the stomach and the baby started laughing. Aiden smiled with him. Ben calmed down and went back to staring. He poked Ben in the stomach again and Ben started laughing once more. Their game went on for a while. Aiden thought he would grow bored, but he didn't. He imagined what it would sound like for somebody to call him Dad. Aiden checked his cell phone and he noticed he had a text message. It was from Clarence. *Blues Concert is in three days. Call me back if you're free.* Aiden thought intently about going. He thought of Richard too. He dialed the minister's number.

"Hello?"

"Hey, sir."

"Why are you calling?"

"I wanted to apologize for how a treated you. It wasn't your job to comfort me. You did it because we were friends or at least I think we're friends."

"It's alright."

"I really need somebody to talk to. I won't try and argue with you."

There was silence on the other end.

"You'll have to wait…"

Aiden's smiled.

"Thank- you."

"Yeah… You know Aiden…You were right. I couldn't answer your questions. I've been thinking a lot about the stuff you said. I don't know what my own opinion is."

"You'll find it, you just need to have faith."

Richard laughed.

"Now you're making fun of me?"

"I would *never* be so blasphemous."

"I'll see you later. Where should we meet?"

"I'm at the house babysitting. Can you come over?"

When Aiden hung up he felt impatient. Ben wasn't much of a hassle. Boredom and waiting felt worse than just about anything. He remembered there was a time when he was good at waiting. It was a time when he had no responsibilities. When he didn't care about the future, but now when he wasn't doing anything he felt aggravated. It was time to find work. He grabbed a newspaper, the latest edition. He flipped to the side with the local jobs section. He surveyed and wondered which occupation he would be best at. Occupation. That wasn't the best word to describe what he would be doing. An occupation was something you went to college for, but a job a teenager could do is not an occupation. Aiden continued to look despite his growing frustration. Cashier. Janitor. Garbage man. What the hell were all these. All this strife and he might end up cleaning puke off the bathroom floor at Wal-Mart. Aiden's anger boiled over.

"Damn it... Don't tell your mother I said that in front of you."

Ben stared wide eyed at him. Aiden continued looking through the paper, and he decided maybe he could be a cashier. He was never good with math. Most modern boxes were just big computers anyway, but Aiden was never very good with computers. He kept looking, and Aiden looked down when he heard soft snoring. Ben was asleep. He wasn't sure what he was supposed to do, but he picked up the toddler carefully and carried him to Deirdre's back room. He placed him gently in the crib. He thought about everything he had ever heard about childcare. What was he supposed to do when they were asleep?

Aiden knew he couldn't put a blanket over him. Babies would smother themselves. Aiden also knew he had to watch him constantly to make sure he didn't try to get out of the crib. Aiden started to curse Deirdre. Why had she trusted him with this... *thing*? Ben continued snoring, and Aiden didn't feel so frightened. He thought about having his own son. He could do it. There were so many pitfalls in parenthood. So many responsibilities... But he was curious to watch something grow. Something that looked so much like him. That would be... Aiden walked away from the crib. He looked back at Ben to make sure he was okay and turned off the light.

Aiden saw Deirdre had a baby monitor. He grabbed the Walkie Talkie- like device. He made sure everything was working properly. He was never good with technology. He left the room and left the door open a crack. Aiden sighed. He started to tip-toe quietly trying to not make the slightest sound, but the floor boards creaked and Aiden winced yet there was no crying coming from where Ben was sleeping. Aiden wiped some sweat from his brow. He made it back into the living room and he breathed again. There was a knock at the door, and Aiden cringed. Ben started wailing.

Aiden sighed. He lumbered over to the door his head hanging low. He opened it prepared to do a lot of shouting, but he saw it was Richard and Aiden smiled frustrated at nobody but himself. He moved out of Richard's path and allowed him inside. Richard nodded and came indoors. He had snow on the shoulders of his black wool coat and on top of his grey wide brimmed hat.

"You can sit on the couch, I'll take your coat and hat."

Richard thanked him, and Aiden put the wool coat over his arm. It was much heavier than he thought it would be, and damp. Aiden took Richard's hat in his other free hand. He put his coat and hat on a rack by the door. Ben was still crying. Aiden smiled at Richard.

"I'll just be a minute." He quickly found Ben and tried to quiet the infant. "I'm here. Don't worry. I'm here."

Ben stared wide eyed. Aiden smiled, and Ben started to relax again. The infant closed his eyes. Aiden sighed and returned to the living room. He sat in the recliner.

"I see you've been looking for work." Aiden saw Richard was looking at the newspaper on the coffee table. Aiden nodded. "You can always take my job."

"You look exhausted."

Richard looked up at him with one eye open and one eye half closed

"…So do you."

Richard pointed a finger. Aiden didn't respond. Richard was breathing heavily, and Aiden thought it might be from the weather or maybe something else…

"What are you thinking of doing?"

Aiden shrugged.

"Nothing at this point seems like a choice. This place belongs to my girlfriend. She's taking care of a child, and I'm just wallowing here, and I'm losing it…" He looked at Richard and saw that there was something in his demeanor which was different. His shoulders were slumped and his face sagged. "What's up with you?"

Richard gave a cynical laugh.

"There's been a lot of violence on the streets recently. I've had to talk with a lot of grieving families, and it's taken its toll. I think I might quit..."

Aiden frowned and looked away.

"I'm sorry for dragging you out here."

Richard smiled.

"Aiden... Nothing you've been through is insignificant. We've all got problems, but some people don't seem to realize I've got my own."

"Yeah, but you don't need me laying my grief all over you on top of everything you have to deal with."

Richard shook his head.

"You're a friend, Aiden, not a church member. I feel like I can be more honest with you than anybody else." Richard stood up. He went to the rack and took off his wool coat and hat. "I do have to be leaving. I know I just got here, but I wanted to check up on you."

Aiden nodded. Richard sighed and started to leave. He looked outside. It was snowing. It always was. He looked back at Aiden. "My wife left me and took the kids. Says I've been too distant. She can't stand it. I suppose she's right... Aiden. I have faith. That's what's keeping me going. What's keeping you going?"

"Hope."

Richard nodded. He walked out and closed the door behind him. Aiden continued looking through the newspaper. The rest of the day was uneventful, but Aiden got up and made himself and Ben a couple of meals. He played with Ben some more. Ben spoke a few words, but most of the time it was gibberish. Ben liked to move around. He knocked into a wall a couple of times. Aiden winced the last time he did it. Aiden thought about intervening, but when he did Ben started running all over again. He was like a little wind-up toy. Aiden figured Ben would have to learn on his own. Ben became tired again, and Aiden put him back in the crib. Deirdre came home not long after, and in her hands were Styrofoam containers.

"We're going to have leftovers for dinner."

"Aren't we special?"

He helped her inside. He even took off her coat.

"Aren't you a gentleman?"

"I try."

Aiden and Deirdre went to the kitchen.

"How is the little one doing?"

"He's asleep."

"...And the world didn't fall apart!"

Aiden rolled his eyes.

"Actually he did very well."

"Don't you mean *you* did very well?"

"Of course I did. Was there ever a doubt?"

Deirdre opened the containers, still smiling.

"So did you do job searching?"

"YES!"

Deirdre jolted back. Aiden hadn't meant to be so loud. He was excited though.

"Sorry. I want to be a cashier."

Deirdre nodded. She took out a chicken breast and put it on Aiden's plate. He stared at it for a while.

"You don't like chicken?"

"No, I just ate."

I can put it in the fridge.

Aiden smiled.

"It'll be good for later." Deirdre put it away. She started walking to her room. "Be quiet. Ben's still asleep."

Deirdre scoffed.

"He's *my* kid, Aiden. I know what to do." Aiden nodded. She went inside, and she came back out with Ben still in her arms. His arms were limp against her chest and he was still asleep. Deirdre walked into the living room and Aiden followed her. She sat down on the couch and Aiden did too. He looked over her shoulder. Ben was snoring softly. "I really love that sound; I can't fall asleep without it now." Aiden smiled and nodded. Deirdre's face became serious. "Did you want to talk about your friend?"

Aiden's stomach curdled then he sighed.

"Truth is, I didn't really know him that well. I've never been to his house. I never knew who the other people are he interacted with... There is this other man I talked to. *Still* talk to. I have the same problem. I was talking with him, and I never knew the problems he had to deal with."

Deirdre reached over and held Aiden's hand. He looked out the window.

"It's snowing."

Deirdre smiled.

It always is.

Tuesday February 27th, 18 days left

Aiden's back was stiff. He had been sitting in the back room of the nearby dollar store for about ten minutes. He kept looking at the time on his phone. The room was a cold cellar-like space with four brick walls and an old ceiling fan circling above. He stretched and heard a couple of bones crack. A woman came in and Aiden tried not to slouch, but his posture had never been very good. She was a large woman with red curly hair and she sat in a seat across from him looking at a clipboard. Aiden straightened his tie. The woman inspected him with one eye. The other eye looked like it was trying to exit her face. She looked like a chameleon with her eyes going in different directions like that.

"Have you ever had any work experience before?"

Aiden didn't know what to say. He had been a bouncer at Bartley's bar for the past twenty-five years? Aiden lowered his head.

"No."

She scribbled something on her clipboard.

"What makes you think you'd be good at this job?"

Aiden hated questions like that.

"I'm really old." He said with a laugh. The woman wasn't laughing. Aiden stopped. Aiden lowered his head again. "I've got experience, but I don't plan on doing anything else. I'm not going to mess around like a cocky teenager. I'm reliable and I'll always be here on time. I'll do anything you ask." The woman nodded. She scribbled more down on the paper on her clipboard. She looked at the clock. Aiden stood up and she stared at him. Well... stared at him with *one* of her eyes. Aiden felt guilty for insulting her for her looks even if it was inside his own head. He didn't look too good himself, but he was nervous and the woman wasn't being friendly. "So, when should I call you?"

"We'll call you."

Aiden nodded. He started walking out. As soon as he got outside he ripped off his tie and he contemplated throwing it in the trash, but he kept walking. Deirdre was sitting in her truck when Aiden got inside.

"How'd it go?" She looked and saw his face. She touched him. "It'll be alright." She started to pull away from the curb. Aiden looked out the window. He looked for the sun. Dark clouds rolled above, but he couldn't see any light. "They said on the radio we're going to have showers mixed with snow." Aiden didn't respond and Deirdre took a deep breath. "It'll be okay, Aiden."

"You said that."

Ben was at daycare and Deirdre stopped to pick him up, but Aiden waited in the car. She told him she wouldn't be long and left the keys in the ignition when she went inside. Aiden turned on the radio and closed his eyes and let the melody sweep him away far from his problems. Deirdre came back out and interrupted his splendor. She put Ben in the back seat and Aiden turned around to look at the toddler. Aiden waved and Ben smiled. He had bright rosy cheeks.

"I think he's happier when he's around you."

Aiden figured she was just saying that, but it lifted his spirits. She pulled out of the parking lot of the daycare and they were home within a few minutes. Aiden offered to carry Ben inside, but Deirdre watched carefully from the side. Aiden unbuckled the car seat. He hadn't expected that Ben would wrap his arms around his neck. Aiden's eyes opened wide and he stood up excitedly. He turned around to show Deirdre and she laughed. "Yes... I see." They went inside. Deirdre opened the door for Aiden. He walked in and plopped down on the couch. He dropped Ben beside him. "You want the chicken? Deirdre asked walking passed."

Aiden nodded. He returned his attention to Ben and he started to play a game of Peek-a-boo. Ben clapped his tiny hands with excitement.

"More." Aiden pretended to get bored and turned away; Ben tugged on his sleeve. "More."

Aiden would continue. Ben grew tired of the activity. Aiden urged him to play more, but Ben resisted. Deirdre came back out with the plate of chicken.

"If the toddler grows bored before you do then I think it's time to try a new game."

Aiden scoffed.

"What do you know?"

Aiden suddenly jumped off the couch and ran into the kitchen and Ben followed.

"Aid-ee?"

It was Ben's butchered pronunciation of Aiden's name. Aiden jumped out and Ben tried to scamper away. Aiden snatched him up and put him on his shoulders. Ben screamed with delight and Aiden went and sat back down on the couch. He let Ben down who crawled back into his mother's arms.

"Oh, so now you want me? Are you hungry?" Ben nestled his head deeper into her arms. She sighed and stood up. She went to the kitchen. Ben followed her. "Are you going to keep looking for a job?" Aiden didn't want to talk about it. Deirdre came back out. Ben followed closely behind her ankles and in his hand was a stalk of celery that he nibbled on. "It's okay."

"No it's not. I'm here leaching off you. You should be furious."

Deirdre walked a couple more steps and sat next to Aiden on the couch. She held his hand. She lifted it up to her mouth and kissed his fingers.

"I believe you can do it."

Aiden smiled. As much as he could smile. Ben came and crawled in between them. His stalk was on the floor. Deirdre moaned and gave a weary laugh. She picked it up off the floor, and grimaced at the slobber that dripped on her hand. She plucked a hair of the frayed end where Ben had been chewing.

"Yours mommy."

Deirdre frowned even more.

"Go on mommy," eat it Aiden mimicked.

Deirdre rolled her eyes at him.

"Eat it mommy," Ben repeated.

She pretended to chew on the end. Ben laughed. Aiden thought anything could make Ben laugh. Deirdre went back into the kitchen and threw out the celery.

"I'll help you look, Aiden. I have friends who can help you search for a job. If all else fails you can work at the Tavern with me."

Aiden chuckled. Then he sighed.

"I just wish I was rich so I could buy you pearls and fur coats."

"Oh, what a romantic!" She sat next to Aiden and gave him a hard look. "Do you really think I care about those things?"

Aiden shrugged.

"Maybe it's not for you, maybe it's for me. I just want something out of life. I feel like I've damn well earned it."

Aiden realized Ben was in the room.

"Sorry."

Deirdre ignored the remark.

"How much has your life improved since you been with me?"

"A hell of a lot."

"Damn straight, and that's just because I'm the most perfect human being, isn't it?"

Aiden rolled his eyes. He couldn't think of anything clever.

"Right."

Deirdre started laughing.

"Come on Aiden, cheer up."

He gave one eye to her. The other eye was closed.

"I got nothing to be cheery about."

"Not even my magnificent presence."

Aiden groaned.

"I swear Deirdre; you can drive a man insane."

She laughed and kneeled on the couch. She pecked him on the cheek. Aiden leaned over and grabbed her. Deirdre laughed. Aiden put his arms on either side of her. Deirdre was under him looking up with her doe-like eyes.

She looked like a cat on her back. Aiden closed his eyes. Deirdre touched his face. For a second Aiden wasn't sure where he was. He opened his eyes again. He was disoriented. Deirdre was still looking at him.

"Do you want to go somewhere?"

"Where?"

Deirdre pursed her lips.

"We could go out to eat."

"I'm not hungry."

"We could go to the park."

"I've been to the park."

Deirdre thought harder.

"We could go to the beach."

"What are you planning to do at the Beach?"

"Walk on the boardwalk."

"What about Ben?"

"We'll take him with us."

"Can you leave like that?"

"I got nothing else to do."

Aiden sat up.

"It's a bit spontaneous."

Deirdre shrugged. She sat up to and put her arm around Aiden.

"Then let's be spontaneous. Get Ben ready."

She got off the couch and went to her room. Aiden looked at the toddler. The toddler looked back.

"You got a crazy mother, you know that?" Aiden smiled at Ben's blank expression. "Don't you ever grow up, don't do it. Being young is the best part of your life." Aiden went to Deirdre's room. She handed him some of Ben's cloths. "I haven't been to the beach in decades."

Deirdre shrugged.

"It's a pretty nice place."

"Are you sure you don't have anything else to do today? This isn't normal."

Deirdre walked over to him and kissed him on the lips.

"Stop worrying and have some fun."

Aiden gulped. What did he have to fear? Aiden went back out into the living room and dressed Ben. The toddler started kicking as Aiden began undressing him.

"Will you hold still?"

Ben became still. Aiden put on his diaper, tiny blue jeans, and shirt. Deirdre came out with a packed bag.

"You know the beach is two hours away. Are you sure you want to go?"

Deirdre groaned and threw her head back.

"Aiden, I know this is unusual, but will you just go with me? We haven't anything else to do. It'll be fun."

Aiden thought he knew the meaning of that word at one time.

"I'm sorry for being cynical. It's in my nature. It's just that… it's not you. I'm that way with everybody. I keep hearing people tell me to lighten up. I think I might actually try it."

"Stop being so melodramatic, you're ruining everyone's good time!"

Aiden laughed and nodded. They walked out the door and Aiden carried Ben over his shoulders. Ben was gleaming with excitement even though he had no idea where he was going. They got into the truck, and Deirdre pulled out of the driveway. Aiden turned on the radio, but Deirdre turned it off.

"Wait until I pull out." The street was quiet. Aiden didn't know what she was complaining about. They drove in silence until they got onto the highway. "Can you imagine when we start teaching Ben to drive?"

"I really don't want to think about it."

Aiden nodded and looked out the window.

"We should go swimming when summertime comes."

Deirdre nodded.

"I used to really like swimming, but I hated getting all sandy. It was much more fun when I was younger."

Aiden raised an eyebrow

"So I guess you're not as much of a free spirit as I had believed?"

"You think I'm a free spirit?"

"We're going to the beach in February out of the blue."

Deirdre nodded.

"Yeah, I guess that's true. I'm a free spirit when I don't have to get dirty." She looked at Aiden. "When are you a free spirit?"

"When I'm with you, sugar pie."

Aiden leaned in for a kiss, but Deirdre rolled her eyes and pushed his face away. Deirdre turned on the radio. Aiden looked out the window. An hour went by quickly when listening to music. He watched the scenery pass. This would be the first time he had left the city since… the cabin. Aiden wiped some sweat off his brow and turned up the music.

Deirdre stopped at a gas station. Aiden went inside to buy himself a snack. He asked Deirdre if she wanted anything, but she shook her head. The man behind the counter when Aiden went inside was huge. Six foot four at least and well over three hundred pounds, but mostly fat. Aiden got some chips and a soda. He paid with some cash in his back pocket, but he was using up the last of his cash. He needed to find a job and soon. He hoped he would have enough to spend on this trip with Deirdre. He walked back outside and Deirdre was back in the front seat waiting for Aiden. She smiled at him and Aiden smiled back. The anxiety still swirled in his stomach. He took a sip of his coke, but it didn't help. Deirdre got back onto the main road.

"What did you get? I want one."

Aiden tried to guard his food.

"I offered to get you something."

Deirdre reached over.

"Dang it, Deirdre!"

She grabbed the chip and swerved during the scuffle.

"Thank you Deirdre; now we are all going to die."

She laughed triumphantly and put the chip in her mouth. She focused on the road and turned back onto the highway.

"Oh, you can't afford it anyway. I'll be buying all your stuff."

Aiden knew she was joking, but the comment still stung. He became quiet and Deirdre knew she had said something wrong. She frowned at him.

"I'm sorry, I didn't mean…"

"It's okay."

Aiden knew Deirdre hadn't meant to hurt him. He felt guilty for snapping. It was after all his own fault he didn't have a job.

"I know you weren't trying to say anything. I just am a little sensitive right now."

Deirdre shook her head.

"It's okay, Aiden. You'll find a job."

"No! It's not okay. You've done everything in this relationship. I need to step up, and I'm afraid I can't."

"You've been taking care of Ben. That's more than anybody else has done."

"Ben's a good kid. I'd do anything for that child. Any decent person would."

Deirdre was quiet. She looked away.

"Not every person has. Just you. I don't know where Ben's father is."

"He was a scumbag."

"Then what are you complaining about? You're the best thing I've ever had."

"…But I'm not the best thing you deserve."

Deirdre leaned over and kissed him. Aiden had his arms folded and looked like a pouting child.

"Try not to kill us."

"I only swerved a little bit that time."

The majority of the ride was quiet. Aiden was listening to a song he had never heard before. Deirdre rolled her eyes when she saw him moving to the beat.

"It's a stupid pop song."

Aiden shrugged.

"I was listening to the melody."

"You got to listen to the lyrics. He's just talking about how pretty some girl is that he met in a café. How much he's in love with her, even though he's probably seventeen. He doesn't know what love is."

"How old do you have to be to love somebody?"

"I don't know, but old. It's also got to do with how long you've been in a relationship."

"How long have we been dating?"

Aiden knew it couldn't have been too long and Deirdre knew it too.

"Okay, you got to be old and it's got to be longer than over a course of a weekend. Otherwise it's just lust."

"When did your lust for me turn into love?"

Deirdre laughed.

"You're not exactly the prettiest."

Aiden pretended to be hurt.

"You've ruined my dreams of modeling."

"You do have lovely eyes."

"Why, thank you."

"...No, I think you've got to have at least one fight before you love somebody."

"Really? So then you must really love me?"

"Damn straight!"

Aiden snorted. Deirdre started laughing too. She laughed so hard that she was barreling over and her head touched the steering wheel.

"Jesus Deirdre, it wasn't that funny!"

Deirdre kept shaking her head back and forth.

"I know."

She was still laughing hard. She was shaking. She swerved.

"Jesus!"

They drove for another half-hour before they reached the beach. It was empty like Deirdre had predicted.

"Can you get Ben?"

Aiden happily obliged. Ben was asleep. When he woke up he blinked a few times and Aiden unbuckled him from the car seat. He put Ben up on his shoulders.

"You ready to go?"

Aiden nodded.

"I was talking to Ben."

"Oh."

Deirdre had a half smile on her face. She made a strange look at Ben and Ben gave a small laugh. They walked a few blocks before coming to the beginning of the boardwalk. They passed a few shops.

"Did we drive two hours just to look?"

"Yeah."

"Oh, okay."

Deirdre stopped to get some food from one of the vendors. She bought two hotdogs and she gave one with mustard to Aiden. Aiden broke off the end and gave a piece to Ben. They continued walking, but stopped and Deirdre bought a beer. She urged Aiden to drink, but he refused.

"Seriously?"

Aiden nodded. Deirdre put the bottle near his lips.

"Just a sip?"

Aiden backed away.

"No."

Deirdre sighed. Aiden bought a root beer. Aiden stared at the waves. Deirdre looked where he was staring.

"You want to walk on the beach?"

"It's freezing."

Deirdre tugged on his sleeve.

"We won't go into the water."

Aiden groaned, but followed her. They threw their empty bottles into a nearby recycling bin. He put Ben down who was still bundled up. Aiden stood up and he felt something cold and wet smack into his face. He looked around and saw Deirdre traipsing around him. Are you like, twelve? There was still sand clinging to his cheek. Aiden kneeled down and started to make a ball of his own, but Deirdre started running away.

"NO!"

Aiden aimed. He adjusted for his moving target. He swung his arm and released the ball from his fingers.

Deirdre covered her face with her hands. Aiden tried to scoop up another handful of snow, but before he could stand back up, Deirdre charged and climbed on his back. Aiden pretended to try and throw her off him, but they both fell into snowy sand. They were both laughing and breathing heavily. Aiden started to clean Deirdre's hair. He pulled out clumps of sand and snow. Deirdre looked serious.

"Where's Ben?"

"He's right over there."

Deirdre looked where Aiden pointed and saw Ben digging a hole. She looked calmer, but then she looked nervous again.

"He's going to eat it."

"No he's not."

Deirdre got up and picked up Ben. Aiden walked over to her. Deirdre bought a few more beers later in the evening and returned to a spot in the sand to watch the waves. Ben was between the two of them.

"Isn't this romantic?"

"It's cliché; I got sand in my butt. How Lancaster and Kerr did it I'll never know."

Deirdre slapped him on the arm.

"Stop it and enjoy yourself."

Aiden smiled and put his arm around her. The water came closer and closer to their feet.

"I want to take off my shoes."

"It will be cold."

Deirdre smiled.

"I'm going to do it."

She put her socks into her sneakers, but she was shivering.

"I told you so."

She screamed and clutched tighter to Aiden's side.

"I feel like we've known each-other long enough to call you an idiot."

"What are you so scared of? You think that our wet toes are going to give us hypothermia?"

"Probably."

He took off his own shoes. He grinded his teeth and waited for the cold water to come. Aiden shivered, but when the water retreated he realized he had overreacted. They sat for a while watching the sun sink into the horizon.

"We should probably head back."

"I know. I want to wait here just a little bit longer."

Ben was asleep in the snowy sand.

"The boardwalk's closing."

"I know."

"You look worse than Ben."

She looked at him. A strand of hair was in her mouth. She pulled it out and pointed a finger at Aiden. She was about to talk. Would it be clever?

"Shut up."

Nope.

"Let's go."

Aiden grabbed her hand and hoisted her to her feet. She swayed. Aiden grabbed her beer bottles. Five in all.

"I think I'll drive."

They stumbled together through the night, but before they were in the first ten feet of the vehicle Aiden had to catch Deirdre. She had collapsed, and it was made all the more difficult because he was carrying Ben too, but Aiden put her arm around his neck and started to drag her forward. He opened the passenger side of the truck and tried to sit her up straight, but she flopped over. Aiden lifted her back up and thought he had gotten her still. He closed the door, and she collapsed again. Aiden rubbed his forehead. He put Ben in the car seat in the back.

Aiden started driving, and tried to wipe the tiredness out of his eyes. He tried to remember how Deirdre had got to where they were, but once he got onto the highway the drive became easier. He drove straight for forty minutes and then took the exit and he knew where he was. Finally, Aiden pulled into the driveway of their home. He took Ben into the house first and then he got Deirdre. He carried her over his arms like a groom carrying his wife down the aisle… or like a monster carrying a woman in one of those nineteen fifties B-films. He watched her for a minute or two before he went back outside to shut the truck door. When he came back in he sat down on the recliner. He picked up the newspaper and started reading the help wanted section.

Friday March 16th, 2 days left

"Hello, Mam. Is that all you would like to buy?"

The old woman nodded, but she didn't smile. Aiden never knew someone so old could be so unfriendly. He didn't say anything. He just kept smiling at her while she counted each individual penny from her purse. A few patrons... customers, Aiden had to stop thinking of them as patrons. He wasn't at a bar, he was in a clothing shop. The other customers showed their frustration visibly. Aiden would have to calm them down without upsetting the old woman. It was a balancing act he wasn't very used to and he looked over his shoulder to see the store manager watching everything he did. It was Aiden's third day on the job.

"If you wait I'm sure another line will open very soon."

The woman didn't seem to recognize the growing unhappy crowd behind her. Aiden didn't know if she were partly deaf or partly blind, but probably both. She wore massive thick rimmed glasses and hearing aids. When she had finished counting her change she handed over the pile to Aiden. He thanked her and deposited the change into the cashier box.

"... Now I just have to get my coupons."

There was a loud moan from the crowd. Aiden wished he could be amongst them, but instead he had to stand perfectly straight and keep smiling. The woman was quicker this time with her search, but it really didn't matter because by that point another lane had opened. The other cashier was Andrei. A young kid Aiden had befriended. He was a bit of a hippy-dippy type, and Aiden had no doubt he was on some sort of substance at any given moment, but Aiden liked him. He was always smiling and friendly. He had been doing the job that Aiden was just learning for over five years. It was no mystery why he turned to drugs or maybe he was doing a job like this because he was on drugs, but either way Aiden didn't care. The store manager came over. He was an individual who Aiden cared less for. He was balding and skinny and he never walked. He had an angry trot. His arms were stiff at his side.

"Did you get everything handled?"

Aiden nodded. He looked down at the man. There was a smudge on his nametag so that the Y in Larry didn't appear. Instead it said Larr. Aiden knew it was a small detail, but he kept focusing on it.

"Are you listening to me?"

Aiden shook his head.

"I'm sorry?"

"I need you to work late today."

Aiden nodded.

"Okay, sir."

He had wanted to go home. He knew Deirdre would be home by now. She had been doing her job for a while. She had been able to gain a lot of control over her schedule, but Aiden wasn't so fortunate.

"You'll be here until eight?"

Aiden nodded again.

"Is that understood? I want to hear you say it?"

"Yes, sir."

Larry…or *Larr* always demanded to be called sir. The employees called him different things behind his back. Larr started to stiffly trot away.

"Hang in there dude."

Aiden smiled.

"Thanks."

Aiden kept thinking of Deirdre. It had been two weeks since the beach. He had been through so many interviews, but he got better. A lot better. He knew exactly what the employers wanted. He had to swallow all his pride. He looked out the window of the store. It was snowing as it always was, but Aiden wondered if Deirdre was home curled up on the couch with Ben. He liked the thought. He stood up again ready for the next wave of customers. There was nobody as awful as the elderly lady, except for one business woman. She made him and others wait while she talked on the phone. When Aiden tried to interrupt her, she put her finger up. Aiden bit his tongue. He thought he tasted blood. After her, the day was almost over. Aiden had been standing for hours. His legs were beyond tired and they threatened to buckle. He looked at a clock on the wall. His phone had to be turned off. He hated that rule. He wished he could call Deirdre once an hour to make sure she was alright, but instead he waited for his break in the middle of the day. He had a half hour to talk and eat.

"How are you?"

"Good."

"How's your job?"

"…Good."

"Really?"

"…Yeah."

She would talk about Ben, and Aiden would listen. He didn't need to reply. He was just glad to hear her voice. He wanted to be curled up in Deirdre's arms with Ben playing with his toys at their feet. Aiden stopped daydreaming and went back to work, but Larr approached him.

"You can go home."

"What?"

"I said you can go home."

Aiden nodded. He was too tired, but he felt some sort of joy. He'd never experienced this sort of joy. What was it? It was a nice tired. Aiden had gotten a new car. Now that he had a job he felt he could spend some of the money he had left from working for Bartley. It was a hybrid. He laughed at himself and immediately showed it off to Richard. He had even grown attached. The small vehicle had its charms to Aiden's surprise. Snow was a problem, but springtime was close or at least that's what the weathermen kept promising. He figured that's when he would use it most, but during the winter he would use Deirdre's truck.

The roads were icy, but they had been plowed. Snow in March. What a fucking joke. How screwed up can this weather get? He continued driving without incident. He stopped at a red light and he looked around. He saw a girl and her father cross in front of him. She was skipping in bright red boots into the puddles of partially melted snow. Her father scolded her when some muddy water splattered on the bottoms of his pants. The light turned green. Aiden waited for the daughter and father to pass before he continued, but the car behind him honked. Aiden kept smiling blissfully unaware. When the father and daughter were off the street, Aiden put his foot on the gas. It wasn't long before he pulled into Deirdre's driveway.

Aiden got out and quickly raced to the door. He slipped. He groaned while he laid there for a moment looking up at the sky as snow fell. He imagined he was a turtle that had been flipped over. He looked at the door and it opened. Deirdre came out. Was he dying? He saw Deirdre laughing. She gave him a hand and Aiden supposed he wasn't.

"Did you salt?"

Deirdre shook her head.

"I've been relaxing like you've been urging me to do."

Aiden shook himself. He stretched his back and a few bones cracked.

"I hope you fall on your ass so I can laugh at you."

Deirdre was still smiling.

"Come in I made you soup."

Aiden was immediately greeted by the warmth. He stood for a minute letting it all soak in.

"Close the door."

Aiden didn't listen. She grumbled and walked around him. Aiden hung up his leather jacket after she shut the door. He went to the kitchen and sat at the table. Deirdre's home was a lot cozier since Aiden had moved in. There were pictures on the wall, a colorful carpet on the floor, and they had even painted the walls a calm blue. It was chicken noodle that Deirdre had made. He tried to use as much restraint as possible, but he desperately wanted to slurp the contents of the bowl. He picked up the spoon and delectably brought the broth up to his mouth.

"I've taught you well. You're civilized."

It was like she was reading his thoughts. She rested her elbow on the table, and her chin on her knuckles. She was surveying him and Aiden looked back at her.

"I've made you human. I'm the one who got you to make this place feel less like a mental institution."

"You're being awfully hyperbolic."

"Oh, somebody's been reading the dictionary."

Aiden looked around

"… Where's George."

"I haven't seen him."

"That's not good."

"He'll turn up."

Aiden finished scooping the last mouthful of broth. Deirdre took the dish away and rinsed it out in the sink.

"Do you want to watch a movie?"

"That would be nice."

They went out onto the couch and curled up together. Ben was on the floor playing with blocks. Deirdre put on an old comedy show Aiden had never seen before, but he enjoyed it with her. Deirdre pressed her head against Aiden's chest and she listened to his heartbeat.

"You seem calm."

Aiden brushed her hair with his fingers.

"I am with you."

Deirdre looked up and kissed him. Aiden's calm was fleeting. His muscles ached and his head throbbed.

"I'm going to take a nap."

"Why?"

Aiden sighed.

"I just need to relax."

Deirdre didn't argue, but she wasn't happy. Aiden went to the bedroom and shut the door. He took off his shoes and pants. It was dark, but Aiden pulled down the shades and climbed into bed. He put his hands under his head and stared at the ceiling. He heard a buzzing. He woke up, but there was nothing. He relaxed on his back for another half hour struggling to fall asleep. What was wrong with him? Why wasn't he happy? He was when he left his job and he was when he got home. What had changed? He had wanted to see Deirdre for so long, and now that he was with her he felt... disappointed. George jumped up on the bed.

"There you are."

George settled down next to Aiden's hand.

"I suspect you want me to pet you?"

The old cat purred. Aiden started scratching the feline behind the ear. He got up and George meowed, but Aiden went back into the living room. He watched Deirdre. The old comedy show they had been watching was coming to an end. He leaned against the wall.

"I have tried so many times being somebody else. It isn't working. I'm too old."

Deirdre laughed.

"Too old? You're wearing long black socks, white briefs, and a white undershirt."

Aiden gave a half smile and started to walk away.

"Where are you going?"

"I'm going to go for a drive."

"You can't go for a drive naked!"

"I'm getting dressed!"

He went to the bedroom where Deidre and he slept. He grabbed the lighter from the desk beside the bed. He emerged wearing jeans and a black T-shirt. He walked over to the closet to retrieve his black leather jacket.

"Where are you going?"

"I just need to clear my head. I'll be back."

"What's bothering you?"

She looked ashamed.

"It wasn't you. It was a lot of things not least of which has been my job."

He opened the front door and Deirdre shivered. Aiden thought the cold felt good. It stung his cheeks, but it made him feel alive. He stared hesitantly across the spot where he'd fallen. He walked with trepidation hoping the same accident wouldn't occur twice. Aiden got into his car and he sat for a minute with the engine off. Snow was piling up on the windshield. Aiden turned the key and pulled out onto the quiet road. He was heading for the park. He turned on the radio. Aiden felt more relaxed. It didn't take long before he could see the woods. There weren't many people around. Aiden got out of the car after he'd parked and started running and he kept running until he was under the bare branches of the forest. He slowed his pace. He felt better. Deirdre was far away. Aiden didn't know what had come over him. He had waited all day to see her, but now he needed to be alone.

He reached the spot beside the river where he had killed the prosecutor. Where he had met Clarence. Where he had dumped his father's ashes. There he saw a man. Aiden saw him from the back and as he walked closer he noticed the man looked more familiar.

"Richard?"

The man in the black wool coat turned around. He had a bottle in his hand. He smiled at Aiden and Aiden walked over to sit down next to him. Richard's hair was a mess or at least the couple hairs that remained, and he swayed even though he was sitting.

"What happened to you?"

"I got drunk."

Aiden sat down next to him. Richard looked intently at the river and Aiden looked with him.

"You know the world is getting better."

"Really? There are problems in the Middle East, problems in Eastern Europe, and problems here at home."

"…But as a whole the world is getting better. We're entering peace times."

Richard paused. He thought for a moment and took another swig of his drink.

"We've had peace times before until war breaks out again. War, peace, war, war, peace. It's monotonous. I think the desire for violence is in the human DNA."

Aiden tried to retort, but eventually agreed.

"We can try. We can rise above our natural instinct. We can get better."

"Are we lucky enough to get better? One mistake and we'll blow each other up. I think humanity might be doomed… There was a man, who was struck multiple times by lightning, and I heard somebody comment, well it was bound to happen to somebody. If I were the man who had been struck by lightning I would be horrified. That statistically speaking, getting struck multiple times was bound to happen to somebody, and there is nothing I could have done to prevent what had happened!"

"I hate the word inevitability; given enough time, anything that can happen will happen at least until everybody dies. That sounds awful, but maybe you're right and maybe we will destroy each other."

They stared at the river in silence. The ice had melted further and the river had widened. Richard took another sip of his bottle and realized it was empty. He turned it upside down and shook it. A couple drips came out from the rim. He threw the bottle in the river.

"The river is so polluted, but everyone just takes dumps in it."

"Sorry."

"You have caused the least damage. I've certainly littered many times, but I'm guilty of so many things that letting my trash go is not that important."

"What have you done?"

"I've ruined so many lives. I've ruined my own, and in my pursuit of happiness I'm probably going to ruin others."

"You really think you're going to hurt other people."

"Not intentionally not anymore, but I'm trying to leave behind everything I've done, and I thought if I did that I could be redeemed or I'd be fulfilled, but I didn't stop doing what I did for the good of the world. It was for the good of myself and I've never done anything that wasn't in my own self-interest."

"You sure about that?"

Richard struggled for sobriety. He blinked a couple of times. He tried to look sympathetic, but his mind was groggy. He tried to maintain his balance, but Aiden didn't care. He just nodded.

"Nothing feels right, but I keep thinking that things will get better, and they don't. I know the reason now. I shouldn't be living this life. I'm going to end it. It's the only way. I have to end it sooner or later. It's not my happiness I should be worried about. It's that of other people, and the only way I'm ever going to feel content... that's the word. Content. Not happiness, but satisfaction. The only way I will ever be satisfied is if I pay for the things I've done... I'm going home, you going to be okay?"

"I think I'm just going to sit here for a while."

He was still staring at the river when Aiden started walking away.

"You know what you're doing?"

"No. This is going to end badly and I'm going to hurt a lot of people. It won't be easy. I'm giving up everything I've ever wanted... or ever will want."

Richard groaned and held his head as a migraine birthed. He leaned over. Aiden saluted him and started walking.

"Don't do it, kid. It'll get better!"

"Not for me."

Aiden looked up at the black sky and he smiled faintly. He thought what he was doing was right. He got into his car, but he left the radio off and drove in silence. He let his mind wander. The world appeared still. People were out, but not many and they looked like they were moving in slow motion. Aiden passed several stores some of which were closing. Aiden stopped at a crosswalk and let an old man pass. The man's back arched till it looked like he was trying to form the letter r with his body. Aiden wondered what it must be like at that age. He knew he would never be that old. He didn't know if that was a bad thing. He thought it was and it made him want to reconsider. There were a whole host of things that made Aiden want to reconsider.

He kept driving after the light turned green. He passed a bar and Aiden pulled into the parking lot. He sat for a moment. He sighed and got out. He walked in and sat on a stool. The bartender asked him what he would like.

"The strongest thing you got."

The bartender looked at him funny, but he complied. He returned with a small glass filled with yellow liquid. Aiden took a deep breath. He picked up the glass and drank the beverage in a single gulp. It tasted like mouthwash and his tongue was on fire. He coughed and pounded his chest, but the bartender smiled.

"Good stuff, right?"

Aiden nodded and the bartender got Aiden another glass.

"More."

"Another."

"More."

"Anofer."

"Mork."

"Anoder."

Aiden got off his stool and tripped his way to the door.

"Have a nice night sir."

Aiden nodded back. He got into his hybrid. *I'm good enough to drive.* He pulled out too quickly and nearly smashed into the car behind him. Oops. Aiden got back onto the road. He drove about thirty minutes going in circles. Inebriated as he was he was going to die, and it was no use trying to ignore that fact. He thought about it for a few seconds. He wondered what death was like. He wasn't considering an afterlife, but he was thinking about the actual process. He supposed it was all a matter of how you died. If it was a mortal injury then there would be a lot of pain. No doubt that's what would happen. Aiden's death would be slow. He pulled over and started to cry. He couldn't stand the sound of his own weeping. He couldn't stand it! He turned on the radio. It was Louie Armstrong's What a Wonderful World. Aiden started laughing. He started driving again.

He stopped at Deirdre's house. He didn't pull into the driveway. He remained alongside the curb and he sat for a moment staring. It was time to say goodbye. He walked carefully remembering where he'd fallen. He opened the door and he saw Deirdre sitting on the couch watching TV half asleep. Aiden coughed and Deirdre turned her head.

"You feeling alright?"

She was lounging comfortably. Her voice was calm and she looked like she was ready to go to bed.

"Well come inside, your letting all the warm air out."

Aiden smiled and came in, but he left the door open. He stood still staring at her. He smiled, and then he stopped.

"I'm leaving Deirdre."

"Already? You just got here."

She returned her attention to the television. She was watching some cheesy soap opera and Aiden shook his head.

"I'm *leaving*."

Deirdre froze. She almost looked frightened.

"What?"

"I'm *leaving*."

"Oh."

It hardly seemed as if the word had left her mouth. Her face crinkled and folded in on itself like burning paper. Tears poured down freely. There wasn't any noise at first. Just silent grief. He heard her snort as she tried to breath. Aiden wanted to comfort her. He walked over as scared as he was, but as soon as he got close she slapped him. He didn't try to dodge her blow. It had stung him more than he realized. All the drunkenness he had felt was gone. He didn't touch the red mark on his face. He kept looking at Deirdre. She tried to cover her face. She looked ashamed.

"It's alright."

He tried to put his arms around her, but she pushed him away. She got off the couch and pushed him again.

"You promised me!"

Aiden thought the neighbors might call the police.

"You promised me!"

Aiden was backing out the door. He continued backing up until he was outside. Deirdre tried to hit him again, but Aiden caught her wrist. He had to restrain her and he held her close. It looked like they were about to kiss. What a Wonderful World was still playing in his head.

"You make me want to live, Deirdre, but I can't. I'm a murderer."

Deirdre's eyes widened and her skin became as pale as the winter sky.

"No, that... No."

"It's true, Deirdre. I've killed men, women, and children. I was paid well, and sometimes I enjoyed it. Where do you think I got the money for the car?"

Deirdre struggled out of Aiden's arms. She ran into the house, but she slipped and fell on the floor. She started crawling away and it looked like she was screaming, but no sound was coming out. She shut her eyes and looked away.

"Go."

"Deirdre..."

"GO!"

Aiden stood still looking at her. Her words bashed against him like a cold wave. He glanced back at his car. He looked back at Deirdre who was still on the ground cradled up.

"Alright, Deirdre."

Aiden started walking away. He stopped on the last step of the porch. Louie Armstrong's voice popped into his head. What a Wonderful World. He sighed, and got into his hybrid. He pulled back out onto the street and he thought humorously how difficult it was to look sad in such a dinky car.

He continued driving and parked his car near the curb across from the woods. He got out of his hybrid and walked to the bench where he killed the prosecutor, where he met Clarence, where he dumped his pills, where he dumped his father's ashes, where he disposed of his mother's picture. He listened to the wind blow. The branches shook, twisted, and whined. Aiden sat motionlessly like he was part of the environment. He listened to cars driving in the distance. He was surprised there were people still out. He looked at the time on his watch. It was half passed four in the morning. Had time gone so quickly? He started dialing Quinn's number.

"Quinn?"

"Aiden?"

"You want to come and meet me. I got to talk to you about something."

"What?"

"I'll tell you when you get here."

Aiden thought he heard Quinn drink something. He could only guess what it was.

"Yeah, I guess I could show up. Got nothing better to do."

"I'll see you then."

Aiden had the notepad and pen in his hand. He started making a list of names of all the people he killed. It was a difficult task. He had tried to forget their faces for so long. *You should turn yourself in.* If I live then I will. *You're not going to live.* No? *You're afraid of living.* Probably. *You're going to hell.* I know. Aiden made a duplicate list. He figured his task was complete, but then he ripped out one more piece of paper.

Deirdre. Aiden sighed. He put the pen down. What could he possibly say? *Deirdre I love you.* No, that wasn't right. ~~*Deirdre I love you.*~~ *You make me want to live Deirdre.* Aiden tilted his head back and forth. That could work. *You saved me, and I promised I wouldn't ruin your life. You took me in. You were scared of being betrayed. I lied to you. Please forgive me.* No, that wasn't good. ~~Please forgive me.~~ *I don't deserve to be forgiven. Remember Ben. Please, he needs you. You can't give up. You have Ben. I had you, but I walked away. You're stronger than me. You can't abandon people because you get scared.* Aiden stopped. ~~You can't abandon people because you get scared.~~ *I'm am the worst form of a hypocrite. I've been thinking a lot about inevitability. We make things inevitable. What I am doing is all me.*

Aiden grew aggravated. He crumbled it up and tossed it on the ground. He heard a car door shut. He turned his head sharply. He put his notepad and pen on the bench next to him. He heard footsteps scuffing against the pavement. He saw the outline of a man emerge from the darkness. The moonlight ran like water over his silhouette. Aiden saw it was Quinn, but he had a bottle in his hands.

"Is everybody in this city a drunk?"

Quinn shrugged and he let the bottle slip from his fingers and smash on the ground. Quinn continued walking uncaringly. He leaned himself against a tree and looked down at Aiden.

"… So what did you want?"

Aiden stood up so he could look Quinn in the eyes. He gave a subtle sad half smile.

"I'm going to confess."

"Confess what?"

His lids were drooped low and his eyes were red and puffy, but it didn't seem like he would be able to comprehend much of what Aiden was saying.

"I'm going to give the police a confession."

He waited and watched to see if Quinn now understood. Quinn furrowed his brow.

"You can't do that!" He started shaking his head back and forth. "You can't do that. I'm out."

"I'm out too. We still have to pay for what we've done."

Quinn shook his head. He started pacing. He was breathing in short quick bursts.

"No Aiden. That's you. You want to confess, go ahead, but leave me out."

"It's the right thing to do."

Quinn became stiff and his eyes got wide.

"I won't let you."

Aiden started to chuckle, but tried to hide his smile with his hand.

"Come on, Quinn. You're not thinking straight. You're drunk."

"No."

Aiden was still smiling. Quinn produced a revolver. Aiden stopped smiling. He raised his hands. Quinn was crying.

"I don't want to do this. I've done so many shitty things. I just want to quit."

"You can't."

"Bullshit! You tried."

"I failed."

"Well... I won't."

"Quinn..."

"Ah, Fuck."

Quinn put the revolver under his chin and pulled the trigger. Aiden flinched before he heard the blast. He heard the body collapse on the ground, but Aiden still didn't open his eyes. He couldn't see and he wished he could go blind, but then he opened one eye, but it wasn't out of curiosity. He simply wasn't afraid anymore. Quinn was coughing. His eyes were open. He wasn't dead yet. Quinn was still staring at Aiden. He was shaking. His neatly combed hair was a mess. Aiden knelt down. He brushed a strand out of his face. It had stuck to the sticky surface of his sweaty forehead. Quinn started crying. He clutched Aiden's arm.

"It'll be alright." Aiden failed not to weep. "You're doing fine."

Quinn smiled although tears were still coming out of his eyes. Some of Aiden's own tears splashed on Quinn's forehead. Aiden laughed and turned away. "Sorry."

Aiden wanted to say something, but what? Quinn's fingers loosened around Aiden's arm and his hand fell to the ground. Aiden had stopped crying. He could feel warmth on his back. He turned around and he could see the sun in the horizon. He waited for a while. It was snowing, but Aiden didn't notice. Aiden shook his head. He had to focus.

He grabbed Quinn's hands and started to pull him into the river. He supposed he could have pushed him, but Aiden somehow figured pulling him would be more dignified. He went into the water as far as his knees. Quinn floated for a while, but then sank. Aiden was glad he wasn't a floater. He crawled out of the river. He supposed he didn't have to hide the body. He was ending it all today anyhow, but Aiden was too exhausted to think. It was a funny feeling. It wasn't like anything he had felt before. He was more tired than he had ever been in his entire life, but he felt good. He looked up at the sky, and it was snowing.

Saturday March 17th, 1 day left

"Hello, my name is Aiden. I'd like to confess to murder."

Aiden never thought much about protective custody. He didn't mind if he were dead. So far as he concluded, he was already dead, but he wasn't depressed about his life anymore. In fact he felt alleviated, but what was there to do? They put him in a cell before Bartley's trial. He stared out some bars at the world outside. The sun was shining, but there were still clumps of snow on the ground. It wouldn't remain much longer. As tightly as winter clung there was just no way to avoid the overbearing sun. In a few more days it would officially be spring. Aiden had used to think spring was overrated, but he looked at the world differently now. The guard standing in front of Aiden's cell wasn't a large man. He was young and slightly smaller than Aiden, but he had an intimidating demeanor; maybe it was the way he stood or the stern face he wore.

"How long have you been a cop?"

Jeffery turned his head to look at Aiden.

"Three years."

"Have you always worked in the city?"

"No. I'm an outsider. I guess they figured I'd be untouched."

"I hope so."

Jeff chuckled. The side of his body was partially draped in shadow like a black cloak. He had a buzz cut and looked like he might have been in the military. His stiff disposition had relaxed and Aiden was glad he didn't have to spend the next couple hours with a statue. He had a spark in his eye that Aiden admired and his smile was youthful and energetic.

"How old are you?"

"Twenty six."

"How has the job treated you so far?"

"Good. A lot more gray then I thought there would be. I've seen a lot more good in people since I've become a cop. I got to tell you people aren't as bad as you'd think."

"That so?"

Jeff nodded.

"I guess the most important thing I've learned is that, if you want to make this city better, you got to work with people. You can't just condemn everyone as evil if you do that and you've already lost."

Aiden got off his cot and walked closer. He leaned against the cold metal and stuck his face through the bars. He was staring at Jeff and Jeff took a step back almost wary. Aiden gave a subtle smile since he knew there couldn't be too much confidence in young blood. There was always a little bit of fear for the first few years or so. Aiden had never been a cop, but there were some similarities between his profession and law enforcement. The first connection obviously was the possibility of Death. It took a long time for the fear of Death to scrub off, but after killing so many people the fear of Death intensifies, and then subsides until Death becomes nothing more than a nuisance. Fear of Death transforms into the welcoming of it.

"Have you ever seen someone die?"

Jeff looked confused. He stared at Aiden for a while, but shook his head.

"Thankfully no. I've known others who have killed."

"Have you known any officers who have been killed?"

"No. Thankfully."

"So what do you think happens after people die?"

Jeff shrugged.

"A black void. Disintegration of consciousness."

"You don't think that's cynical?"

"I think it makes life here more special. Sad for people who didn't do anything with their lives, but that's the price they pay."

"What about people who don't have a life through no fault of their own."

"Fortunately I don't think the universe is so cruel. Most people have the chance to better their lives. Most suffering in the world comes from people making bad decisions."

Aiden couldn't argue with that looking back on his life. He sighed and sat back down on the bed. He leaned against the cold concrete cell wall and looked back outside. The sun was still shining and he would be let out later today when they transferred him. He had been guarded closely by a rotation of guards. He was never able to really get to know any of them not that it mattered since he wouldn't see any of them again. He heard they'd be taking him upstate, but he still wasn't sure exactly where he'd be living.

A female officer poked her head in as Aiden was trapped in his thoughts. He turned his head to look at her. She was a thick framed woman with a butch face and blond hair tied up in a bun in the back of her head. Aiden squinted for a moment to make sure that she was in fact a woman. She wasn't looking at Aiden though. She was looking at the other officer. That was one thing Aiden hated since he had been in the hands of the police. He was treated like a non-entity. It was no different than how police usually treated him, but he figured since he had been helping him they'd be a little nicer.

"Bartley is going to testify soon."

"You think he'll crack?"

"I doubt it. Bartley's too smart for that."

Aiden became confused. The woman shut the door, and Aiden looked back at Jeff wondering what their conversation had meant.

"How do you know of Bartley?"

Jeff remained casual.

"Bartley's been under suspicion for a while, but he's always been careful."

Aiden relaxed and put his head against the wall.

"I guess he trusted the wrong people."

"I guess so."

Aiden looked outside again. He could see a bird land on the grass. It started pecking at the ground. It had recently rained and worms had emerged from the soil. Aiden didn't know much about nature, but he thought that coming to the surface could only make it easier to get eaten. There must have been a purpose. What reason did the worms have to reveal themselves? Aiden shook his head. He looked back at Jeff.

"You got a family?"

Jeff nodded.

"Got a wife. We engaged last year. Got a boy and a girl. Three and four."

Aiden smiled.

"That's nice."

Jeff gave a half smirk and put his hands on his hips. He was looking down. He put his hands in his pants pocket and pulled out a pack of cigarettes. There were only two left in the cartridge. He took one of them and stuck it in the side of his mouth. He lit it and took it out of his mouth so he could blow a cloud of smoke. He offered Aiden one, but Aiden refused. Jeff shrugged and leaned against the concrete wall staring up at the ceiling.

"You got kids?"

Aiden shook his head.

"Never wanted any."

"Why?"

"Didn't think I could hack it."

Jeff laughed.

"Not so hard once you know what you're doing… But I'm glad."

"About what?"

"That you don't have any kids."

"Why?"

"Cause it probably be harder with your life."

"True."

Aiden was quiet again for a while. He was looking aimlessly in the distance thinking about the future. Where would he be? He would have to start a new life. Who would he start it with? He didn't know if he could put himself out there again. He had done so well with Deirdre, but losing her he had also lost his strength.

"You ever think about the future?"

Jeff's eyes widened. He took his cigarette out of his mouth. He looked confused, but then he nodded. He gave a complacent smile when he looked at Aiden. He put the cigarette back in his mouth. He paused before speaking.

"My children. My legacy. That's what drives me. My wife. It's being a provider. That's how I define myself, but for everyone it's different. You got to find meaning in your life. It might not be the same as somebody else."

"You got a lot of wisdom for a... how old were you? Twenty six?"

"Yeah."

"Could I get that cigarette now?"

Jeff reached into his pocket and pulled out the cigarette. Aiden put it in his mouth and Jeff lit the end. Aiden sat back and relaxed.

"I never drank. Never wanted to, but smoking was fine. Prescription medication was fine. Hypocritical I know, but drinking affects your mind, and that's what I was scared of. I've known people who got lost to the drink. It does crazy shit to the mind."

"Yeah."

"... You sure we're allowed to be smoking?"

"There is a lot of things I'm not supposed to do."

"Like what?"

Jeff shrugged still looking relaxed.

"You got to understand it was all for my kids."

Aiden became confused.

"Like what?"

Aiden's guts began to slither in his stomach like snakes. Jeff standing over him started to sweat, and Aiden dropped his cigarette.

"Shit."

Aiden lunged up and attempted to subdue Jeff, but surprise was not on Aiden's side. Aiden was old and Jeff though shorter was younger, healthier, and stronger. He bent low and grabbed Aiden around the waist. He hoisted Aiden up and threw him on the ground. Aiden's head smacked the floor and he could feel warm blood trickling down the back of his neck. Aiden lying on the ground resorted to kicking Jeff's knees in a pathetic display reminiscent of a child's form of fighting. Jeff began walking around and when Aiden kicked out he grabbed his legs and twisted his foot. There was a snap and Aiden screamed.

"HELP! HELL...!"

Jeff began to silence him by kicking him in the sides and in the face. Aiden rolled over and began to curl up. There were no more blows after Aiden ceased to fight back, but Aiden looked up and he could see Jeff pulling his gun out of his holster. Aiden sat up and crawled to the back of the cell. He was still looking at Jeff who appeared in no hurry to kill Aiden. There was a look of sadness on his face. Aiden began to laugh.

"That cat is going to outlive me."

"What?"

"Nothing..."

"How do you intend to convince others that you didn't kill me?"

"Bartley's empire has crumbled for good thanks to you, but you know Bartley wasn't going to go down until somebody was dead."

"I know."

"No you don't. Bartley's not just going to kill you."

"Deirdre?"

The words didn't escape his mouth without his throat becoming syrupy. Jeff kept shaking his head back and forth. Aiden's face became red hot and he started to sweat.

"No. Please. I have to protect her. Please…"

"Oh, stop. Can't you die with some dignity?"

Aiden looked out the Plexiglas of his cell. It was snowing as it always was. A snowflake landed on the window. Jeff squeezed the trigger three times. Two bullets entered Aiden's chest and another went through Aiden's neck. If he hadn't of been so close Jeff was sure he would have missed. His hand was shaking uncontrollably. He dropped the weapon as soon as the job was finished. It landed with a thud on the ground. Two police officers entered the room. Jeff's mind was so frozen he didn't attempt to resist. He was still staring at Aiden's body as they arrested him. One of the officers was a blonde haired woman. She leaned close to his ear.

"You got him good."

"Yeah… Yeah I did."

www.ingramcontent.com/pod-product-compliance
Lightning Source LLC
Chambersburg PA
CBHW071150260626
47162CB00003B/993